A whoop went up from the small band of Indians emerging from the scant cover of a rise, and Jennings spun around at the sound.

Britten saw the workers running toward him, many of them carrying guns and some even firing past him toward the onrushing Indians. He dropped out of the saddle and joined the growing line of resistance, jamming more shells into the Starr and then blasting away at the howling savages.

The whistle on the locomotive let out a piercing shriek. Combined with the rattle of gunfire, it let the entire camp know that something was wrong, and more and more men appeared, guns in hand.

"The Indians are pulling out," Britten told them. "I guess they decided they were outgunned."

But the construction boss did not looked so relieved. "They'll be back with a lot more braves."

Britten did not reply, but he was afraid Jennings might be right. No matter what had brought it on, the short truce was over.

They were headed into trouble now, real trouble.

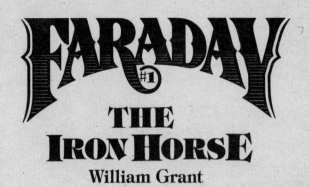

FARADAY #1

THE IRON HORSE

William Grant

BCI™ Created by the producers of
**Wagons West, Stagecoach,
Badge,** and **White Indian.**

Book Creations Inc., Canaan, NY · Lyle Kenyon Engel, Founder

LYNX BOOKS
New York

FARADAY #1 - THE IRON HORSE

ISBN: 1-55802-181-7

First Printing/July 1988

Produced by Book Creations, Inc.
Founder: Lyle Kenyon Engel

This book is published by Lynx Books, a division of Lynx Communications, Inc., 41 Madison Avenue, New York, New York, 10010. The name "Lynx" together with the logotype consisting of a stylized head of a lynx is a trademark of Lynx Communications, Inc.

Printed in the United States of America

0 9 8 7 6 5 4 3 2 1

FARADAY #1

THE
IRON HORSE

Prologue

AT FIRST THERE WAS ONLY PEACE ON THE GREAT PLAINS.
Far in the distance, across seemingly endless miles of
gently rolling prairie, a dim blue line of mountains
could be seen on the horizon—the mountains that
marked the beginning of the majestically upthrust
Rockies. A vagrant breeze soughed across the plain,
making the grass wave lazily. A prairie dog poked its
head up from its burrow and scanned the surroundings, its nose and ears alertly seeking any sign of
danger.

The little creature ducked frantically back into its
hole as it heard the sounds of approaching death.

A moment later a horse thundered over the burrow,
its hooves narrowly missing the entrance. A misstep
would have sent the big animal head over heels,
spilling its rider.

Carl Duncan leaned far over the horse's neck,
urging his mount on to greater speed. The wind
whipped Duncan's face, blowing his long brown hair.
His heart was lodged firmly in his throat, cutting off
his air—or at least that was how it felt. Fear had his

pulse pounding as loud as the hooves of the galloping horse.

From behind him came the faint cries of the pursuing Indians. Duncan cast a glance over his shoulder and saw that they had closed the gap a little more. And he was already getting all the speed he could from his horse.

Riding southeast over the Kansas plains, Duncan knew that the railhead of the Kansas Pacific was less than five miles away. But that five miles might as well have been five hundred. He would never make it that far before the savages caught up to him.

Then Duncan thought about the telegraph line that stretched from east to west. Though the railroad was still striving to complete a transcontinental route, such a link had already been established by Western Union. If he was estimating the distances correctly, he might be able to reach it in time.

He knew that his own life was probably forfeit, but if he could reach the Western Union line, he could climb one of the poles, tap into the wire with the telegraph key he carried in his saddlebag, and pass along the discovery he had made. It was vital information. If he could get it into the right hands, it might save dozens—even hundreds—of lives.

As he rode desperately, Duncan found his mind going back over the circumstances that had brought him to this dangerous situation. Almost from the first, problems with the Indians had plagued the men who were trying to span the country with rails. The Union Pacific line to the north had had some trouble, but the Kansas Pacific had taken the brunt of the attacks. The surveying crews that ranged far in front of the railhead were the most common targets of Indian attacks, but the tracklayers and work locomotives were also being struck now. The progress of the railroad was being seriously threatened.

And now Carl Duncan knew why.

He corrected himself as he lashed his quirt across the flanks of his laboring horse. He did not really know why the Indians were being stirred into a killing frenzy, but he knew who was responsible for it. A white man. A man Duncan knew . . .

Duncan had been out there in Kansas for several weeks, and in that time he had met many people, but he had had no trouble recognizing the man he had been studying earlier through a telescope. Duncan had bellied down behind a slight rise and used the scant cover it gave him to spy on a meeting between a Sioux chief and a white man. The white man had been laughing and jovial, obviously not fearing for his life. He had given his orders to the Indian, and then they had parted, the chief heading back to the small band of warriors that had accompanied him to the meeting, and the white man back toward the railhead.

As soon as he had realized what was going on, Duncan knew he had to get the information to the proper authorities. He had been riding hard when he ran across a stray group of braves, the ones who now were chasing him. There had been no place for him to hide, and the Indians must have been unable to resist the temptation of a lone white man riding on land they considered theirs.

So the chase was on, the Indians hot on his heels.

The wind in his face brought tears to Duncan's eyes. He blinked them away as he thought he spotted something up ahead. Peering intently, he saw the poles again, jutting up from the plains in a never-ending line, bearing the single strand of iron wire that carried messages from coast to coast, the Western Union line.

Duncan raked the horse with his spurs. He jerked his head around as the weary animal tried to gain a little more speed. The Indians were several hundred yards behind him now, but he still had a chance to get the message through. That was all he could ask for.

His progress over the dry flatland was agonizingly slow. The peeled-pine telegraph poles seemed almost to be receding into the distance instead of getting closer. But gradually they grew in size, until finally

Duncan could make out the thin wire itself against the late-afternoon sky, sagging slightly between poles.

As he approached the line, Duncan reached into his saddlebag and found the telegraph key with the wires wrapped around it. He pulled the apparatus out and had it in his left hand as he hauled the horse to a stop with his right.

Duncan dropped from the saddle even before the animal came to a staggering halt. He raced toward the nearest pole, just a few feet away. The whoops and cries of the Indians came clearly to his ears, but he tried to ignore them.

Shinnying up a telegraph pole was no problem, even with the key to carry. Duncan had some experience in telegraphy, along with quite a few other things, and he climbed steadily, taking his time. Slipping and falling now would mean the end of his chances to pass along his message.

He did not look at the Indians closing in on the pole as he reached the top. Wrapping his legs securely around the wood, he balanced himself as best he could, set the sending apparatus on top of the pole, and began working to tap into the line. His breath rasped hotly in his throat as he performed the task with experienced ease. When the wires of his set were attached to the line, he took a deep breath and began flicking the key on the sender up and down with dizzying speed.

An arrow whipped past his head, and Duncan bit back a curse. So far he had been unable to raise an operator on the line. He was sending blind, with no idea of whether anyone was hearing him.

Another arrow thudded into the pole just below him. He glanced down at the sound and saw the shaft quivering there, less than six inches from his leg. While he continued to operate the key with one hand, he used the other to slip the Navy Colt from the holster on his hip.

Duncan counted six braves in the band that had

chased him there. Four of them were still racing their horses around the pole, shouting their hatred, but the other two had dropped off their ponies and were taking careful aim at him with their bows. Gritting his teeth, Duncan squeezed off a shot at one of them.

He saw an Indian jerk backward as the bullet thudded into his chest. The other brave howled furiously for a moment, then loosed another shaft. Duncan tried to shift his position, but he was too late. The arrow sank deep into the muscle of his thigh, sending waves of fiery pain coursing through him.

Crying out, Duncan clutched the pole desperately, but he felt himself slipping. His right leg did not want to work. In a matter of only seconds his pants had already become soaked with blood. The telegraph key was knocked from its precarious position, but it fell only a few inches before the wires attaching it to the main line caught it.

There was nothing to catch Carl Duncan, however. After firing one more wild shot, he fell from the pole, and as he smashed into the ground on his back, the impact knocked all the air from his lungs. Something snapped inside him, and more pain lanced through his body. A broken rib, he thought. Soon that would be the least of his worries.

The gun had fallen from his hand when he hit the ground, and he saw it lying a few feet away. He rolled onto his side, ignoring the agony in his chest, and lunged toward the weapon. A moccasined foot came down on his hand before he could reach it, pinning him to the ground.

Duncan looked up into a grim red face. The brave had another arrow in the bow, the string drawn back tautly. At this range, the shaft would smash bone and pulp flesh and tear completely through him . . . and he knew that would be the luckiest thing that could happen to him now.

The warrior grunted abruptly and lowered the bow, releasing the pressure on the string and removing the arrow to slide it back into the quiver hung on his back. With his foot still on Duncan's hand, he looked at his companions and snapped an order. Duncan did not understand the language, but he knew what the brave was probably telling them. He groaned, not from pain but from despair.

The Indian stepped back, and a couple of the others jerked Duncan to his feet. They left the arrow lodged in his thigh as they marched him over to his weary horse, his wounded leg threatening to buckle under him. As he was roughly lifted into the saddle, he saw one of the other braves climbing the pole to retrieve the telegraph key.

It was possible they did not know what the instrument was but wanted it only as a pretty souvenir of a foolish white man's death. Duncan hoped that was the case. His sacrifice had a better chance of doing good if the Indians did not know he had been in contact with other white men.

Of course, he had no way of knowing whether that had really happened. The electrical impulses forming his frantic message might have gone nowhere. He would never know for sure—because, he thought as he leaned forward in the saddle of the plodding horse, all that awaited him now was death.

The fires of the Sioux village burned brightly that night, and there was much joy. Shouts of laughter mingled with the shrieks and cries of the captured white man.

The torture had begun with the setting of the sun and had continued for many hours, and the limp bloody form tied between two poles near the largest campfire now bore little resemblance to a man. His eyes had been left unharmed so that he might see what was happening to him, and his tongue was also intact, so that he might scream. But every inch of the rest of him had felt the touch of fire or blade or both.

His lamentations were a good thing—good for the warriors to hear and entertaining for the women and children. The braves hoped he would not die for a long time yet.

The soft sound of hoofbeats approaching the camp went almost unnoticed. Then one of the sentries, his attention distracted by the torture in which he wished he could participate, snapped to alertness as a man rode out of the darkness. A white man in a buckskin jacket . . .

"Put down your bow," the white man ordered in the tongue of the Sioux. "Take me to Black Club."

The sentry nodded, relaxing as he recognized the newcomer. This white man, unlike all the others, was a friend to the Indian and helped the warriors in their battle to drive away the hated iron horse.

Within moments the sentry had taken the man in the buckskin jacket to Black Club, the chief of this band. His arms folded, Black Club stood several yards away from the captive, watching the torture with approval in his dark eyes. The man in the buckskin jacket waited in silence for the chief to acknowledge his presence.

Finally Black Club waved a hand at the captive and said in English, "We caught this man speaking on the devil wire. He has given my men much sport this night."

The man in the buckskin jacket nodded, a frown on his face. "You're sure he was using the telegraph, Black Club?"

The chief made a sharp gesture, and one of his braves produced the telegraph key. Taking the apparatus from the brave, Black Club extended it toward his visitor. "This was on the devil wire," he said. "The man rode like the wind to reach the trees with no branches before my warriors could catch him. Did he speak to the men who bring the evil of the rails to my land?"

Turning the telegraph key over in his hands, the man in the buckskin jacket mused, "That's what I'd like to know." He dropped the key and strode over to the prisoner. The braves who were busily peeling more skin from his body stopped their work and stepped back.

The white man stared at the prisoner in recognition. "Duncan?" he said.

After several seconds, the name must have penetrated the captive's pain-numbed brain. Slowly his head lifted, and his lidless eyes stared with horror. At first there was something like a faint flicker of hope in them at the sound of another white man's voice, but then that died when he saw who had spoken.

"What were you doing out here, Duncan, spying on me?" the man in the buckskin jacket demanded. "You'd better answer, or I'll turn these heathens loose on you again."

When a rasping sound came from the prisoner's throat, the other white man leaned closer, trying to make out the words. He smiled as Duncan repeated, "G-go . . . to . . . hell!"

"Reckon you're already there," said the man in the buckskin jacket. "I can make it easier on you. A nice quick bullet in the brain, Duncan—how does that sound? The chief and his braves won't like it, but that's what I'll do for you. Just tell me who you're working for and if you managed to contact them."

The captive's mouth moved, but no sound came from it. The man in the buckskin jacket leaned closer still, and his smile widened as he realized that Duncan was trying to work up enough saliva to spit in his face.

The man laughed, but he was worried nonetheless. There was obviously more to Carl Duncan than he had thought; otherwise, Duncan would not have been skulking around out there and sending telegraph messages. Had he seen the meeting this afternoon with Black Club?

"You'd better talk, Duncan. Black Club and his men can keep you alive all night if I tell them to. What's happened to you so far will be a party compared to what they can do to you. Just tell me who sent you out here and what you reported to them."

The prisoner suddenly lunged forward, straining at the thongs that bound him to the poles. One blood-slicked hand slipped from its lashings, and he reached for the neck of the other white man.

The man in the buckskin jacket jerked back, and out of the corner of his eye he saw movement as a brave drew back a tomahawk. "No!" the man cried, but he was too late. The weapon flashed through the air and thudded into Duncan's forehead, cleaving his skull. The bloodied form sagged, still held up by the bindings on his other hand, and gray matter seeped from his hideously split head, slowly masking what was left of his face.

The man in the buckskin jacket whirled on the warrior who had killed Duncan. "Dammit!" he exploded. "You didn't have to do that! I was in no danger."

The brave's face tightened in angry lines, and the white man quickly bit back his anger. He was safe here in the camp with these Sioux, but there was no point in pushing his luck.

He strode over to Black Club, concern etched on his face. "Did your men say how long he was using the telegraph before they captured him?" he asked.

The chief nodded. "A short time only. Did the man do evil?"

"Probably not." The man in buckskins sighed. "All we can do is hope that he didn't get through—and be more careful in the future."

That was true. Everything had gone too far to turn back now. But if one person could find out what was really taking place, another one could, too.

The man reached inside his buckskin jacket and withdrew a rolled-up piece of paper, which he held out to the chief. "I came to your camp tonight as I said I would, Black Club, to give you more maps of the route of the iron horse. You can study them and decide where you want your men to strike next."

The Indian took the maps and nodded solemnly.

Then, as the man in the buckskin jacket swung up into his saddle, Black Club asked, "What would you have us do with the body of the prisoner?"

"Let the coyotes have it," the man replied off-handedly, his mind already on other things.

Chapter 1

MATTHEW FARADAY STOOD AT THE SINGLE WINDOW IN HIS Kansas City office and peered out at the beautiful spring day. Weather like this made a man want to get on the back of a horse and leave desks and paperwork far behind. Faraday's sharp blue eyes scanned the great sweep of the Missouri River and the impressive span of the recently opened railroad bridge over it.

He was a tall man, a little over six feet, with broad shoulders and a lean waist. His thick hair was silver and his deeply tanned face was rather craggy, but there was a vitality about him that made his exact age hard to determine. As was his custom, he had shucked his suit coat and yanked loose the tie around his neck. No point in a man being uncomfortable in his own place of business.

Gold letters on the pebbled-glass pane of the outer door proclaimed this to be the main office of the Faraday Security Service, and below that, smaller letters read MATTHEW FARADAY, PRES. Nothing further was needed, since Faraday's clients—the nation's railroads—knew who he was and what he did before their representatives ever set foot in his office.

The door of Faraday's inner office opened, and a small man, who had dark, curly hair and was wearing a suit, entered the room with a sheaf of papers in his hand. As he placed the papers on the desk, he said to Faraday's back, "More reports for you to read and sign, sir."

Faraday sighed. He turned away from the window with a friendly grin on his broad mouth. "No rest for the wicked, eh, Charlie?" His tone was soft and contained just a trace of a drawl.

"No, sir, I suppose not," Charles Roth replied. "I wouldn't know."

Faraday's grin widened. "You don't have even a little streak of wickedness in you, Charlie?"

"Of course not, sir. I'm much too busy. Sinning properly is rather time-consuming, from what I've heard."

Faraday laughed and said, "Then I'll have to give you more time off, won't I?" His hand resting on the back of his chair, he pulled it out from the desk. "All right, I'll get to work on this. Is there any coffee out there?"

Roth smiled slightly. "It should be ready quite soon, sir."

Nodding, Faraday waved a hand in dismissal and then sat down, picked up the report on top of the stack, and leaned back to read the scrawled words of one of his operatives. After a moment he frowned, thinking that it might be a good idea to check the penmanship of any applicants he interviewed in the future. Most men did not have the precise, easy-to-read handwriting of Charles Roth.

Faraday's mind began to wander. Roth had been invaluable in setting up this office. The agency had begun in Chicago, but Faraday had decided to move his headquarters to Kansas City six months ago. As the owner of the only investigative agency in the country working solely for the railroads, Faraday had known he needed to be closer to the frontier. The inexorable expansion of the railroads meant that most of the cases commanding his attention occurred west of the Mississippi.

With the help of Roth and a corps of tough, experienced operatives—some of them hired away from his old friend and rival, Allan Pinkerton—Faraday had made this agency a success. Now, with the steady growth of the railroads, there was sure to be even more work for them, since the lure of big money motivated many unscrupulous men to take advantage of the rail lines.

The sound of a locomotive chugging along the rails came through the open window along with a warm breeze. Faraday got a faraway look in his eyes as he listened. There was something special about trains . . . something that called to his soul. Shaking his head, he picked up his pen, dipped it in the inkwell on one side of the desk, and scratched his signature at the bottom of the first report, setting it aside. As he reached for the next one on the stack, the door to the office opened.

Faraday glanced up, expecting to see Roth bringing him a cup of coffee. Roth stood there, all right, but he held no mug in his hand. He had a surprised look on his face.

"Well, what is it?" Faraday demanded after a moment.

"You've got a visitor, sir," Roth said, his voice hushed.

"Not now." Faraday shook his head and gestured at the pile of paperwork. "I've got too much of this blasted mess to wade through."

"Too busy to see an old friend, Matthew?" a new voice asked from beyond Roth.

Faraday lifted his head, his brow wrinkling. The voice was familiar. "Amos?" he asked. "Is that you?"

Roth stepped back to let a man in an expensive suit move past him. The newcomer had salt-and-pepper hair and a neatly trimmed beard. A heavy gold watch chain was draped across his brocade vest, and a stick with an ornately engraved golden head was tucked under his arm. In his hand was a fine felt hat with a narrow brim and flat crown.

Charles Roth, who was seldom impressed by anything, was watching the man with something close to awe.

Amos Rowland stepped up to Faraday's desk and extended his hand to the head of the detective agency, and Faraday returned the handshake as he rose. Rowland said heartily, "Damn, but it's good to see you again, Matthew!"

Faraday grinned. "And it's good to see you, Amos. Sit down, sit down. What brings you to Kansas City?"

Rowland flipped up the long tails of his coat as he took the chair on the other side of the desk. He placed his hat and stick on a corner of the desk and said, "I live here now. Kansas City is going to be one of the centers of the railroad industry, so where else would I be?"

Where else, indeed? Faraday thought. Amos Rowland was one of the chief stockholders in the Kansas Pacific line and a member of its board of directors. Along with Cyrus K. Holliday and the other founders of the railroad, Rowland had turned a small personal fortune into a much larger one.

Faraday had known him for years, from the time when Rowland had owned a small freight company back in Pennsylvania in the forties. The man's holdings had grown steadily since then, and Faraday guessed that he was worth well over a million dollars by now.

"Charlie, bring Mr. Rowland a cup of coffee, too," Faraday said. "Unless you'd like something else, Amos?"

Rowland shook his head. "Coffee is fine."

As Roth vanished into the anteroom, Faraday opened one of his desk drawers, took out a bottle of brandy, and set it lovingly on the desk. "I have a little something to add to it when Charlie brings us our coffee," Faraday said.

With a chuckle, Rowland nodded. "You never disappoint me, Matthew."

Faraday leaned back in his chair again and regarded the railroad magnate. Although he considered Amos Rowland his friend, he had never done any business with the man and therefore suspected that this was just a social call. He had heard no rumors about anything that would prompt the Kansas Pacific to seek his services.

Roth bustled in with two mugs of strong, steaming coffee and carefully set them on the desk. "Will there be anything else, Mr. Faraday?" he asked.

Faraday shook his head. "No, thanks, Charlie."

Roth hesitated a moment, then went out, closing the door behind him.

"You seem to have thrown my secretary for a loop, Amos," Faraday said. "We're not used to directors from the Kansas Pacific visiting us." He splashed brandy into the cups, then pushed Rowland's across the desk to him. Both men sipped the potent brew, and then Faraday continued. "I take it this is a social call, to let me know that you're living here now?"

Rowland took another drink and then set the cup down on the desk. His smiling face became grim as he replied, "No, Matthew, I'm afraid it's not. I've come to see about hiring you."

Faraday frowned. "If the Kansas Pacific has a problem, you know I'm available to help, Amos. But I haven't heard anything—"

"We've kept it as quiet as possible. That's becoming more difficult, though, what with all of the attention that the press is paying to the transcontinental railroad."

"It's quite a story," Faraday grunted. "Three giant corporations all fighting to lay more track than the others, fortunes won and lost, bad weather and Indians to fight. You have to admit, it's a dramatic opportunity for the journalists."

"Yes, and they can throw the whole country into a

panic if they're not careful," Rowland said angrily. "You know what the completion of a transcontinental route means, Matthew."

"You said you were having problems," Faraday reminded him gently. "Why don't you tell me about them?"

Rowland took a deep breath. "You're right. Ranting about the press is not going to do any good. Simply put, Matthew, those red-skinned bastards are giving us fits."

"Indians? I knew they had been harassing the Kansas Pacific."

"Well, it's gone beyond harassment now," Rowland declared. "Those marauding savages have increased their bloody-handed depredations. In the last few weeks there have been at least a dozen attacks on our men. Not just the surveying crews, mind you, but the trackmen and the locomotives themselves. They've not only killed several of our men, but they've delayed the progress of the line. It's unacceptable, Amos."

Faraday clasped his hands together on the desk in front of him. "Unacceptable because men are being killed, or because the Kansas Pacific makes more money for each mile of track it lays?" he asked bluntly.

For a moment Rowland flushed angrily, and then he shrugged. "Both, to be honest. You know how Holliday is. He's concerned with the finances, and so are the rest of us. But we're not heartless, either. A certain amount of blood is going to go into the building of this road, but it doesn't have to be any greater than is necessary."

Faraday nodded and shoved the sheaf of reports aside. His tone was sympathetic as he said, "I understand the problem, Amos, but it sounds more like something that the army should handle."

Rowland laughed curtly and said, "The army cooperates as much as they can, but they don't even listen to me when I tell them what I think the real problem is. They think this resistance from the Indians is just a random thing, the reaction of any savage to someone encroaching on his land."

"And you don't agree with that?"

Rowland shook his head. "I think someone is deliberately stirring up the Indians against us."

Faraday considered that blunt declaration for a moment, then said, "Do you have a reason to believe that, Amos, or is it just a hunch? After all, the Indians have always resisted the coming of what they call the iron horse."

"I know that," Rowland admitted. He leaned forward, dropping his voice slightly, as if afraid of being overheard. "But now they seem to know what we're doing almost before we do it. They've set up ambushes that were not accidents, Matthew. They know our route, they know the schedule of our work trains, and they know when troops are going to be in the area." Rowland's voice shook slightly with anger as he went on. "We have a traitor in our midst. I'd stake my life on it."

Faraday's eyes narrowed. What Rowland was saying could very well be true. The business of constructing railroads was sometimes a cutthroat one, and with millions of dollars' worth of government grants and subsidies at stake, it was not surprising.

"You think someone involved in the Kansas Pacific's construction is passing along information to the Indians?"

"I'm convinced of it," Rowland replied.

"Why would anyone want to do that?" Faraday asked. He thought he knew the answer as well as Rowland did, but he wanted to hear the man's thoughts on the matter.

"There could be several reasons," Rowland said. He snorted. "I know the Union Pacific would do damned near anything to slow us down. They think they can link up with the Central Pacific first, and if they do, they'll be the most important rail line in the country, and their directors know it. But there are other possibilities."

Rowland paused and reached out to put his hand on the brandy bottle, raising an eyebrow at Faraday. The detective nodded, and Rowland added another healthy dollop of liquor to what was left in his cup. He took a long swallow and then sighed.

"You were saying?" Faraday prodded.

"Do you have any idea just how much land speculation is involved with railroad rights-of-way, Matthew?"

"A great deal."

"An incredible amount," Rowland said. "I'd venture to say that there's more money to be made in such speculation than in the actual building of the road. I'd deny this in court, mind you, but I happen to know that Holliday has made a fortune that way. And, well, the rest of us have benefited, too."

Faraday nodded. He knew quite well what Rowland was talking about. As the route for the railroad was laid out, the government condemned huge sections of land along either side of it, paying high prices to those who owned the property. These rights-of-way were then granted to the Kansas Pacific. The directors of the railroad, prior to announcing the route, made a practice of privately obtaining the land themselves ahead of time, so that they would be the owners of the land that the government wanted to buy. In effect, the government was paying these men enormous amounts of money for the privilege of giving their railroads the property. It was a shady scheme at best, widely known in the industry, but a well-kept secret from the general public. As for the men in Congress who approved such shenanigans and made them possible, many of the lawmakers were working hand-in-glove with the railroad magnates and getting their own shares of the booty.

That was just one of the ugly aspects of the business, Faraday thought. He was not fond of it, but he could do little to remedy the situation. Human nature being what it was, a little graft was perhaps an inevitable price to pay for the benefits that the railroads would bring. And for all of its faults, there was no denying that the race to complete the transcontinental route had galvanized the nation.

But the cost in human lives was another thing entirely.

"Someone could be trying to force us to alter our route," Rowland was saying. "The potential profits on the land deals that would result would be plenty of motive for causing trouble with the Indians." He took another swallow of the spiked coffee, then went on. "Besides all that, there could be something else entirely different that none of us has thought of yet. That's why I want to hire you, Matthew. I want you to get to the bottom of this."

"Was that the idea of your board of directors?" Faraday asked.

Rowland shook his head. "I was the one who suggested engaging your services. But the other directors agreed with me. You'll be working for the entire Kansas Pacific, Matthew, not just for Amos Rowland."

Faraday looked intently at the railroad magnate. "I didn't want to think you came to me simply because we're old friends."

"Not at all. You have quite a reputation in the railroad industry, Matthew. We all feel that you're the man for the job."

Faraday nodded abruptly. "In that case, I'll accept the assignment. I'm not saying I agree with your theory, but I'm certainly willing to look into the matter for you."

"Excellent! I have a bank draft with me. . . ."

Faraday waved off the offer. "I'll have Charlie Roth draw up a contract and send it over to you later. For now, this is all I need." He stood up and extended his hand across the desk.

Rowland returned the handshake firmly, then said, "Now that we've agreed on business matters, I do have something personal to ask you, Matthew."

Faraday lifted an eyebrow and waited.

"I'd like you to come to a party at my house tonight," Rowland went on. "It's a big affair, I'm afraid—Hester's been saying we must show off the new house to all our acquaintances. But you and I will find some time to go over the details of the case. And I'm sure Hester will be glad to see you."

Faraday smiled, pleased at the prospect of seeing Hester Rowland again. He had known her even longer than he had been acquainted with her husband. In fact, before her marriage to Amos Rowland, Faraday had courted her.

That was a long time in the past, however, and the relationship between Faraday and Hester had never really blossomed. What he felt for her now was purely friendship, and he was looking forward to the chance to talk over old times with both Hester and Rowland.

"Thanks, Amos," Faraday said. "I'd be happy to come. By the way, do you mind if I bring along the young man I'll be assigning to your case? I'd like for him to get as much information as possible from you firsthand."

Rowland frowned slightly. "You're going to have someone else conduct the investigation? I thought you would handle that, Matthew."

Faraday looked down at his paper-cluttered desk and laughed. "I wish I could, Amos, and you don't know how much I mean that. I'll be coordinating the investigation, of course, but I have agents to handle all of the fieldwork. Your trouble is out there—" He waved through the window at the plains rolling away to the west across the river. "And that's where my man will have to be to discover the root of the problem."

Rowland nodded, but his expression was still a bit skeptical. "As long as your agent is a good man, that's fine."

"The operative I have in mind will do the job," Faraday assured him.

"That's fine, then. Bring him along to the party." Rowland gave Faraday the address and then said, "We'll expect you around eight." He glanced around the office. "I have to admit, Matthew, that I expected a slightly larger operation, not just two small offices and a secretary."

"That's all I need. I want my people out working, not sitting at desks. It's bad enough that I have to spend my days like that."

Rowland grinned. "You always did like to be right in the middle of things." He clapped his hat on his head and picked up his walking stick. "Good-bye, Matthew. I'll see you tonight."

Faraday said his farewells, and then Rowland went out. Through the door between the offices, Faraday saw Charlie Roth hurrying to open the outer door.

When Roth came into Faraday's office a moment later, he found the detective back at the window. "Are we going to be working for Mr. Rowland, sir?" he asked.

"That's right, Charlie," Faraday replied without turning around. "Draw up a contract engaging our services for the Kansas Pacific, will you?"

"At our usual rates, Mr. Faraday?"

"Of course. And find Daniel Britten for me."

"Yes, sir. Who else?"

"That's all. Just Britten."

Roth nodded absently, then looked up in surprise. "You're going to assign Britten to this case alone, sir?"

Faraday swung around, a grin on his leathery face. "You think that's a mistake, Charlie?"

"Well . . . I suppose not, sir. I mean, it's certainly up to you who you have working on each case. But Britten hasn't ever been out on an assignment by himself."

"I have every confidence in all of my men, Charlie." Faraday nodded forcefully. He truly believed that Daniel Britten would find the real culprit behind the Indian trouble—if Rowland's suspicions were correct.

Chapter 2

A FEW MINUTES BEFORE EIGHT O'CLOCK THAT EVENING, A carriage bearing two men drew up in front of a newly constructed mansion on a bluff overlooking the Kansas River.

Matthew Faraday stepped down from the carriage, and behind him came a smaller, younger man who looked slightly ill at ease in the suit he wore. Daniel Britten was in his middle twenties and about half a foot shorter than his employer. The hair under his dark brown bowler was sandy and slightly curly. Normally his youthful face bore a mild, studious expression, made even more sober by the pipe he frequently smoked.

A groom came hurrying to take the team of horses and lead the carriage around the circular drive that led behind the house. Faraday had caught a glimpse of quite a few other vehicles parked in that area as they had approached. Evidently Amos Rowland's party was well attended.

Britten was studying the mansion as Faraday turned back toward him. "What do you think, Daniel?" the detective asked. "I saw the workers putting this place up, but I didn't know it belonged to my old friend Amos."

"Very impressive, sir," Britten replied softly. "The architecture is reminiscent of the prewar plantation houses of the South and somewhat influenced by the classical lines popularized by President Jefferson."

Faraday grinned wryly. "That's exactly what I was thinking, son. Come on."

The two men were met at the heavy double entrance doors by a liveried butler who took Faraday's Stetson and Britten's bowler. Faraday also gave him their names and said, "I believe Mr. Rowland is expecting us."

"Very good, sir." The butler handed the hats to an attractive young maid, then led Faraday and Britten to another door, which opened into a luxurious, high-ceilinged ballroom. What seemed to be at least a score of chandeliers cast their light on a highly polished parquet floor. The walls were lined with paintings, and in several alcoves were tucked pieces of impressive statuary. A steady hum of conversation and laughter came from the crowd of people as waiters with trays of drinks and appetizers circulated throughout the huge room. At the far end of it, four tuxedoed musicians provided classical strains from their violins.

Faraday, spotting Amos Rowland talking animatedly to a small group of men, started in that direction with Britten close behind him. Along the way the president of the detective agency encountered several men and women who smiled and spoke to him. At any gathering involving railroad people, he was sure to know many in attendance.

A florid-faced man caught Faraday's arm and asked boomingly, "What are you doing here, Faraday? Has Rowland hired himself an investigative agent? A little scandal, perhaps?" The man laughed.

Faraday, suppressing his annoyance, laughed politely and said, "Actually, Luther, I'm here because Amos and I are old friends. I've come to attend a party, nothing more."

"Well, it's a good one," the man declared. " 'Scuse me, I need another drink."

As the boisterous man moved toward one of the waiters, Britten frowned and said quietly, "I'd say that gentleman has already had quite enough to drink."

Faraday kept the smile on his face, but dislike was evident in his voice as he said, "I'd say you're right, Daniel. Come on."

Rowland saw them approaching and broke off his conversation, turning to meet Faraday with an extended hand. "Hello, Matthew," he said. "It's good to see you again. I'm glad you could come to our little housewarming."

"I'm glad to be here," Faraday replied. He knew that with others present Rowland would want to maintain the pretense that he was there only as a party guest. Moving aside slightly to let Britten step up beside him, he said, "Amos, I want you to meet a young business associate of mine, Daniel Britten. Daniel, this is Mr. Amos Rowland."

Britten put out his hand and shook firmly with Rowland. "I'm very glad to meet you, sir," the agent said. "I've heard a great deal about you in my studies of the railroading industry."

Rowland's eyes narrowed for an instant, and Faraday read doubt in them. The rail magnate had to know that Britten was the operative Faraday had said he was bringing, but the young man certainly did not look like a detective. But then Rowland laughed and said, "I'm sure most of what you heard were pure lies, Mr. Britten."

"Oh, no, sir. I know how you were the driving force behind the Chattanooga and Western line, and how you got those roads built in Ohio, and—"

"You do know quite a bit about the railroad business, don't you?" Rowland broke in. "I've always tried to work behind the scenes to a certain extent."

"You'll find that Daniel knows a great deal about many things," Faraday assured him. "That's why he's such a valuable associate."

"Well, I'm glad to know that," Rowland said, and Faraday heard the double meaning in his voice. Then Rowland glanced over and raised his voice. "Norman! Come here, will you?"

A slim man with carefully brushed blond hair and rimless spectacles took a drink from one of the trays and then came over to where Faraday, Britten, and Rowland stood. He said, "Yes, sir?"

"Norman, these two gentlemen are Mr. Matthew Faraday and Mr. Daniel Britten. Gentlemen, this is Norman Dodd," Rowland said, completing the introductions. "Norman is my secretary and personal assistant. I'm sure your man Roth is quite good, Matthew, but Norman, here, is outstanding."

Dodd did not offer to shake hands but instead nodded to Faraday and Britten, saying, "Good evening, gentlemen. If there is any way I can assist you, please let me know."

Rowland chuckled. "You're not working tonight, Norman. Why don't you relax?"

Dodd smiled thinly. "I'll try to do so, Mr. Rowland."

Dropping his voice so that it could not be heard more than a couple of feet away, Rowland said quickly, "We'll all meet in the study later, Norman. I'll want you there to take notes and make sure Mr. Faraday has all the information he needs."

Dodd nodded. "I understand, sir." He moved off, carrying his drink and occasionally taking small sips of it.

"Norman's a bit of a prig," Rowland said to Faraday. "But he's good at his job, like I said." He rubbed his hands together for a moment. "Now, why don't we enjoy ourselves for a while? Mr. Britten, feel free to help yourself to food and drink. Matthew, there's someone else who wants to see you."

Faraday knew to whom he was referring. He grinned. "And I'm anxious to see her."

Rowland took his arm, and the two men strolled toward the rear of the room, where several women were listening to the music. Rowland reached out to touch the arm of one of them and said, "Look who's here, darling."

Hester Rowland turned, and a dazzling smile appeared on her face as she saw Faraday. "Matthew!" she cried softly. "Oh, it's so good to see you!"

Faraday took her hand and, with genuine warmth in his eyes and voice, said, "And it's wonderful to see you again, Hester. It's been a long time."

"Too long," Hester replied, squeezing his fingers between her cool, slender ones.

Faraday had expected her still to be lovely, but he was struck by just how attractive she was. Although she was in her forties, her skin was as smooth and unlined as a girl's, at least at first glance, and her ash-blond hair gleamed in the light. Her large, dark blue eyes were as intense as ever. A white gown that left her shoulders bare was draped around her slender body.

As he smiled at her, Faraday saw small lines around her eyes and mouth, and he realized that she had grown thinner over the years. With some women the passage of time softened their beauty; with Hester Rowland it had slightly hollowed her cheeks and sharpened her looks. She was still one of the most attractive women Faraday had ever seen.

"Hester was quite pleased when I told her you'd be joining us tonight, Matthew," Rowland said.

"Yes, you shall have to visit us often." Hester pressed Faraday's hand again. "How have you been, Matthew?"

"I'm fine," Faraday told her. "My work keeps me busy most of the time, and I have friends here in

Kansas City. I'm glad you and Amos have decided to live here."

Rowland slipped an arm around his wife's shoulders. "And we're happy to be here. It's a fine city, and I'm sure it will grow as the railroads do."

Faraday thought for an instant that Hester had drawn back slightly from Rowland's embrace, though the smile on her face did not waver.

"I believe I'll leave the two of you to catch up on old times," Rowland went on. "I see some gentlemen across the room I need to talk to. You know how it is, Matthew—the demands of business never stop, even at a party."

"Indeed," Faraday replied.

As Rowland walked away, Hester moved closer to Faraday and slid her arm through his. "Walk with me, Matthew," she said softly. "I'd like to show you my garden."

"I'd love to see it," Faraday said. He followed as Hester led the way around the edge of the room to a pair of French doors that opened onto a flagstone patio surrounded by flower beds. Colored lanterns hung in the trees around the patio. As they stepped outside, Faraday felt a warm breeze on his face.

Looking down, he saw Hester smiling up at him, and he felt something he had not experienced in many years. He had considered them to be only friends, but a pang of wanting went through him as he studied her face.

Faraday was relieved when she paused just outside the French doors, still in plain sight of the other party guests. He was unsure that he could trust himself alone with her, and a solitary walk in the garden was not what he needed. All sorts of unnecessary complications might arise.

"You have a lovely place here, Hester," he said. "I was quite surprised when Amos told me you had moved to Kansas City, and even more so when he told me where you lived. I stopped to watch the men working on this place more than once in the last few months."

Hester's smile took on a trace of sadness. "I just hope Amos can be happy here. He has had so much trouble lately. . . ."

Faraday frowned slightly. According to Rowland, Hester knew little if anything about the problems plaguing the Kansas Pacific. It appeared that he was not giving enough credit to his wife's powers of observation.

To change the subject, Faraday smiled again and said, "I'm a little surprised that Amos would leave us alone like this. Doesn't he know that I've just been waiting all these years to steal you away from him?"

Hester laughed, a throaty, compelling sound that struck a chord of desire within Faraday. "You had your chance, Matthew, a long time ago. If things had worked out between us, I might never have become interested in Amos."

Faraday shrugged. "I'll know better next time, I suppose," he said. But he knew there would be no next time. From what he had heard of their marriage over the years, Hester was devoted to Rowland.

A new voice came from behind them. "Really, Mother. Stepping out with a man other than Father is so unlike you."

Faraday turned to see who had spoken. The voice belonged to a young woman who stood in the doorway, a smile on her face. She wore a long gown of dark green silk that matched her eyes, and the light from inside shone on the brunette hair that fell in soft waves to her shoulders. She was undeniably lovely, and she was just as undeniably Hester Rowland's daughter.

Hester flushed, partially in pleasure and partially from embarrassment at the young woman's words. She said quickly, "This is an old friend of your father's and mine, Deborah. Mr. Matthew Faraday, this is my daughter, Deborah."

Deborah Rowland lifted her hand, and Faraday

took it and kissed the back of it, bringing a fresh smile
to her face. "Charmed, my dear," he said.

Deborah stepped onto the patio, a flirtatious twin-
kle in her expressive eyes. "My, what a gentleman!"
she said. "If you don't want him, Mother, I'll take
him."

"Deborah!" Hester exclaimed, unsure of how
shocked to be. "That's no way to talk."

"I'm sure that if Mr. Faraday is involved with the
railroad business, he is accustomed to plain speaking.
Am I right, Mr. Faraday?"

"Well, perhaps," Faraday admitted. "I don't run
into too many lovely young ladies such as yourself in
the railroad business, though."

"You will in the future, sir," Deborah declared.
"The day will come when a woman is in charge of the
nation's leading rail line."

Hester's smile was that of a somewhat indulgent
parent. "Deborah intends to run the Kansas Pacific
someday," she explained to Faraday.

"And why shouldn't I?" Deborah asked. "I'm intelligent, and I have a good education."

Faraday grinned. "Can you cuss out a stubborn
section hand?"

The girl lifted an eyebrow. "You'd be surprised."

Faraday laughed, and as he did so, the thought
crossed his mind that if things had worked out differ-
ently between Hester and him, they might have had a
daughter of their own this charming and beautiful.

It was enough to make a man feel old, he reflected
ruefully.

Suddenly the music coming from the ballroom
changed as the players struck up a waltz. Deborah
moved closer to Faraday and slipped her arm through
his, much as her mother had done a few minutes
earlier. "Do you dance, Mr. Faraday?" she asked.

"I've been known to, but I'm not as young as I used
to be." Faraday's eyes scanned the crowd just inside
the window and spotted Daniel Britten standing not
far away, sipping a drink and talking to a man Faraday

recognized as a civil engineer. He went on. "I see just the man you're looking for, Miss Rowland. Daniel!"

Britten glanced around and saw his employer beckoning to him. He spoke briefly to the engineer, then came over to the doorway.

"Daniel," Faraday said heartily, stepping forward and bringing Deborah with him, "this young woman is looking for someone to dance with her. Miss Rowland, may I introduce my assistant, Daniel Britten?"

As he shook Deborah's hand, Britten said, "I'm happy to meet you, Miss Rowland, and I'd be very glad to dance with you."

Deborah took the arm Britten extended, gave a final smile to Faraday, then moved off with Britten toward the open area where several couples had begun to dance.

"She's a lovely girl," Faraday said to Hester, his eyes still on Deborah.

"Yes," she replied softly. "I don't know what I would have done without her."

Faraday, sensing that something was bothering Hester, turned to her, put a hand on her arm, and said, "It may be none of my business, Hester—especially after all these years—but is something wrong?"

She looked up at him and smiled. "Wrong? Why, Matthew, what could possibly be wrong?" Quickly she went on. "Do you remember that little restaurant in Philadelphia where we used to go?"

"Westingham's?" Faraday laughed. "Who could forget that roast beef?"

They continued their reminiscing, Faraday enjoying the memories that their conversation brought back, but still he could not shake the feeling that not all was as it should be here in this magnificent house on the bluff.

As Daniel Britten moved around the dance floor with Deborah Rowland in his arms, he wondered if he was going to be able to carry this off without making a fool of himself. He was not accustomed to dancing, especially not with the most beautiful girl he had ever seen.

And Deborah Rowland was beautiful; there was no doubt of that. Britten had been intimidated by her loveliness as soon as he had seen her, but he was trying not to show it.

Deborah fastened her gaze on him and said, "You're certainly a quiet one, Mr. Britten. Most young men who dance with me are chattering a mile a minute trying to impress me."

Britten smiled slightly. "To tell you the truth, Miss Rowland, I'm not the most accomplished dancer in the world. It's taking all of my concentration just to remember what I'm supposed to do next."

Deborah's soft laugh sent a wave of strange feelings through him. "Do you apply that same level of concentration to all of your endeavors, Mr. Britten?"

He saw the mischievous sparkle in her eyes. He said solemnly, "Only the ones that really matter."

"Then dancing with me is important to you?"

"Certainly."

"Why? Because you're overwhelmed by my beauty and inflamed by passion?" She was being deliberately scandalous and flirtatious now.

"Your father is a stockholder in the Kansas Pacific, Miss Rowland, and a very important one at that."

For a moment, Deborah looked as if she were going to become angry, but then the dazzling smile broke across her face again. "Touché," she murmured. Changing the subject, she went on. "Do you work for Mr. Faraday?"

"Yes, I do."

"That means you're a detective, too?"

Britten frowned. Faraday had been introducing him as a business associate, but no mention had been made of his being an operative. He was not sure how Faraday would have him answer such a question.

The musicians reached the end of their number,

and the dancing couples stopped and clapped politely. Britten was glad of the opportunity to release Deborah from his embrace and join in the applause.

She was not going to be deterred, however. She took his arm and said, "You didn't answer my question, Mr. Britten."

"Why don't you call me Daniel?" he suggested, trying to stall.

"All right, Daniel. Now, are you a detective?"

Matthew Faraday suddenly appeared at Britten's elbow and smilingly rescued him by saying, "Of course he is, Miss Rowland. But good agents never admit it. Why, Daniel, here, has caught more hooligans and thieves than the entire Kansas City police force."

Deborah pouted prettily. "You're teasing me, Mr. Faraday," she accused. "Daniel is a nice young man, but I'll bet he's your . . . your bookkeeper, or something like that."

Faraday shrugged. "She's too sharp for us, Daniel. Come along, son. I'm sorry, but I've got to steal you away for a few minutes."

"Yes, sir." Britten turned to Deborah. "I enjoyed our dance, Miss Rowland."

"Deborah," she insisted. "And I enjoyed it, too, Daniel."

Britten glanced back once as he and Faraday made their way across the room. Deborah was still smiling enigmatically after him.

Britten took a deep breath. He did not mind admitting he was a bit out of his depth here. He had worked for Faraday Security Services for almost a year, but in that time he had not encountered a situation like this.

In fact, this was the first time Daniel Britten had even been in a mansion such as this one. His father had been a keelboater, hauling freight up and down the Mississippi, and Daniel, along with his brothers, had learned at an early age how to work hard. The long days poling their craft upriver had given him muscles that were deceptively hard and strong. The tedious effort had also given him a thirst for something more, a thirst that had led him to educate himself. He had taught himself to read, and from that time forward every book he had picked up had opened another door. Growing into early manhood, he had saved every penny he could lay his hands on, until he had enough to walk away from the river and never go back. He had continued his schooling, working at whatever jobs he could find in his spare time to pay for it.

The Civil War had come along then, and like so many other young men he had found himself on a battlefield in a strange place, not really sure of why he was there, knowing only that to survive he had to kill other young men for the simple reason that they wore gray and he wore blue. He tried not to think of those days too often.

When the war ended, he headed west, again like so many others. The effort to link the nation with rails had already begun, and he drifted into the great endeavor, working first as a laborer and then, as his education began finally to pay off, as an assistant to a crew of surveyors and engineers. Traveling with them had given him the opportunity to observe firsthand some of the Indians who made their home on the Great Plains, and his fascination with them had grown along with his interests in the railroad. It had seemed inevitable to him that the Indians and the iron horse would eventually clash.

Now, from what Faraday had told him, that day had come with a vengeance—and he was going to be one of those expected to deal with it. The prospect filled him with both anticipation and worry. He had never worked alone on an assignment for Faraday, certainly not on one of this magnitude, and he had never worked undercover, as he was going to do now. But he was determined not to let his employer down. He would justify the older man's faith in him or die trying.

Of course, considering the bloody situation on the plains, that was entirely possible.

As the music began again, Faraday and Britten arrived at a doorway where Rowland and Norman Dodd waited. Dodd opened the door and stepped back to let the others go ahead of him.

They entered the room, a large high-ceilinged study, its walls paneled in dark wood. One side of the room was taken up with bookshelves, while another had two large windows, covered at the moment with heavy curtains. In the center of the room was a massive desk with an armchair behind it, and a smaller desk sat in one corner.

Rowland went behind the big desk and sat down, motioning for Faraday and Britten to be seated in comfortable chairs in front of him. After closing the door firmly, Dodd moved to the smaller desk and took a seat there. Rowland flipped up the lid of an engraved wooden box on the desktop and said, "Cigars, gentlemen?"

Britten shook his head and reached into his pocket for his pipe instead. But Faraday said, "Thanks, Amos," and leaned forward to take one of the thick cylinders of tobacco. After Rowland had selected one of the cigars for himself, both men lit them from the oil lamp on the desk, while Britten struck a match and puffed his pipe into life.

Leaning back in his chair, Rowland said, "I don't think we'll be missed for a while. The party seems to be going well." He shifted his eyes to Britten. "Mr. Britten, I take it you're the agent Matthew is assigning to my case."

"Yes, sir," Britten replied. "I hope my efforts will prove satisfactory."

"I hope so, too," Rowland grunted. "There's a lot riding on this. If the Indians aren't stopped, they might do untold damage to the railroad."

Faraday puffed on his cigar and said, "Why don't you tell Britten what you told me this morning, Amos?"

Rowland nodded. Quickly, he filled Britten in on his suspicion that someone was stirring up the Indians in order to delay construction of the Kansas Pacific.

Britten listened carefully, nodding slightly. "I understand," he said. "You think there's a traitor somewhere among the men working for you, someone who is being paid to cause trouble by either a rival railroad company or someone who wants to alter the K.P.'s route."

"Exactly," Rowland agreed.

"Of course, given the nature of the Indians involved, especially the Sioux and the Cheyenne, you've got to expect quite a bit of resistance from them."

"Not like this," Rowland snapped. "Since this morning, I've received word of new atrocities. Norman, if you please."

"Yes, gentlemen," Dodd said, shifting some of the papers on his desk. "According to a report from the head of construction, the Indians tore up a section of track behind the railhead and derailed a work train carrying crossties that were urgently needed. The savages then attacked the wreck, killing three of our men and doing other damage that resulted in two days' delay at the railhead."

"That sort of thing could happen without the Indians having any inside information," Faraday pointed out.

"None of the other work trains have been attacked recently," Rowland said. "Only the one that would delay us the most."

"Coincidence," Britten suggested.

Angrily, Rowland thumped a fist on the desk. "I don't believe in coincidence, sir. Not in something as vitally important as this."

"Take it easy, Amos," Faraday said. "We've already agreed to investigate. Daniel, here, will be heading west in a couple of days to begin looking into your problem. We'll put things right again for the Kansas Pacific."

Rowland took a deep breath and sighed. "I hope so. I can't even begin to tell you what this railroad means to me."

Before he could say anything else, the sound of a quiet knocking at the door made all four men fall silent and look toward the entrance. The door was already cracked, and Deborah Rowland pushed it open farther, stepping inside with a smile on her face and a large silver tray in her hands. On the tray were several glasses and a bottle of brandy.

"I know you men are probably talking business," she said brightly. "I'll get out of your way, but I thought you might want something to drink. Business can be such a dry subject."

All four men had stood up as she stepped into the room, and Britten moved quickly to take the tray from her. "Let me," he said.

"Thank you, Daniel," she replied softly.

Rowland said somewhat stiffly, "Thank you for the brandy, Deborah."

"Is there anything else you need, Father?"

"If there is, I'll send Norman for it. Enjoy the rest of the party, my dear." The tone of dismissal was plain in Rowland's voice.

As Deborah smiled again and retreated through the door, pulling it shut behind her, Britten thought Rowland had been a bit harsh with her, but then he dismissed the notion. After all, the railroad magnate was under a great deal of strain.

Rowland ran a hand over his face. "Thank God I've been able to keep all of these problems from Hester and Deborah," he said. "I'm afraid they would only worry if they knew how badly things were going." He stood up and extended his hand across the desk first to Faraday and then to Britten. "I'm counting on you, gentlemen. Especially you, Mr. Britten."

"I'll do my best, sir," Britten said. He thought

Rowland did not seem very reassured by the words, though.

In the detective business, like any other, results were what counted.

Before leaving the party, Matthew Faraday made a point of finding Hester Rowland again. Ever since their earlier conversation, a nagging concern about her welfare had plagued him.

He found her near the fireplace, standing beside the massive stone mantel. Despite the warmth of the evening, a fire had been built, and Hester was basking in its heat.

Faraday came up behind her and, laying a hand on her arm, was startled by the way she flinched. "Oh, Matthew," she said, smiling nervously. "You frightened me. I didn't hear you come up."

"The party seems to be ending," he said. "I wanted to say good night."

She put her fingers on his wrist. "Thank you so much for coming. You don't know what it meant to me to see you again after all this time. It's . . . good to have friends."

"Don't you have friends here?" Faraday asked. "You know everyone who was here tonight."

"Amos has business acquaintances, and I suppose in a sense I do, too. But I think you're my only friend, Matthew."

Faraday frowned. "If you're unhappy, Hester, you should talk to Amos—"

Her quiet laugh cut across his words. "Amos has enough on his mind without having to worry about my petty problems. And I suspect you do, too, Matthew." She squeezed his hand. "Don't worry about me. I'm fine. I have this wonderful house, and I have my daughter. What more does a woman need?"

Faraday could not answer that question, though he knew now that something was definitely wrong here. He suspected that Amos Rowland had little time for his wife.

Perhaps Hester would be happier with someone else, someone like—

Faraday thrust that thought out of his head. If Rowland and Hester were unhappy, that was their business. He was a man of honor, and he would die before he would take advantage of a friend's unhappiness.

Faraday lifted her hand to his lips. "Good night, Hester," he said.

Chapter 3

THE LOVELY IMAGE OF DEBORAH ROWLAND'S FACE WAS still in Daniel Britten's mind when he entered Faraday's office the next morning. Although he had spoken with her only for a few minutes while they were dancing, he found that she was haunting his memory.

Charles Roth looked up from his desk as Britten came through the door. "Good morning, Britten," he said. "Mr. Faraday is expecting you."

"I know." Britten hung his hat on one of the pegs just inside the door. He had selected a broad-brimmed, flat-crowned hat for this morning, a Western style rather than the bowler he had worn the night before to Rowland's party. He was also wearing boots, brown whipcord pants, and a tan shirt with no tie. The outfit was much more comfortable for him than the suit of the previous evening.

Roth got up and knocked softly on the door of Faraday's private office, then opened it. "Daniel Britten is here, sir," he announced.

"Send him in," came Faraday's booming voice.

The head of the detective agency stood up as Britten

entered the room. Grinning, Faraday waved a hand at the chair in front of the scarred old desk. "Sit down, Daniel. We've got a lot to talk about."

Britten settled himself in the chair as Faraday sat down. His boss was his usual rumpled self this morning. Britten had never known anyone like Matthew Faraday. The man was at home practically anywhere, from an ornate ballroom like Rowland's to a hell-on-wheels railhead settlement. Faraday could handle just about any of the jobs involved in running a locomotive, and he was just as comfortable on the back of a horse.

Not for the first time, Britten wondered if there was anywhere Faraday had not been, anything Faraday had not done.

The silver-haired man leaned back in his chair. "Well, Daniel," he began, "now that you've had a chance to think about what you heard last night, what's your impression of Amos Rowland and his problem?"

Britten hesitated. He knew that Faraday and Rowland were old friends, and he did not want to say anything that would offend his employer.

As if sensing what Britten was thinking, Faraday said sharply, "Be frank with me, son. Sentiment's got little place in the detective business."

Britten nodded. "All right, sir," he said, reaching into his pocket for his pipe and tobacco pouch. He began to fill the bowl. "I'm not convinced that Mr. Rowland is correct in his theory about a conspiracy against his railroad."

"Neither am I."

"But there is a good enough chance that he's right to warrant an investigation."

Faraday nodded. "My thoughts exactly. If there is a traitor working for the Kansas Pacific, he has to be rooted out, for the good of the nation as well as the company." Faraday watched Britten intently as he went on. "Are you sure you don't want me to assign another agent to work with you, Daniel?"

"It was your idea for me to work alone and undercover, sir," Britten reminded him.

"I know that," Faraday said. "But I've been considering it since last night, and I've had some second
thoughts on the matter."

Britten sat up straighter. "Are you afraid that I can't
do the job?" he asked bluntly. The lines of his face had
gone taut with anger.

Faraday laughed abruptly, startling the younger
man. "I didn't say that," Faraday declared. "I thought
you might have doubts. I can see now that you don't."

"I'll do my absolute best, sir."

"I know you will, son." Faraday's strong chin jerked
in a nod. "All right. For now you'll play a lone hand."

"Thank you, sir."

"Just don't let me down, Daniel." Faraday's gaze
was penetrating. He continued. "Now, your cover
identity will be that of a draftsman working with one
of the surveying crews. Think you can handle that?"

Britten nodded as he lit the pipe. "It's a job I've
done before, for real."

"I know that. And it'll give you an excuse to be at
the railhead, as well as to scout out ahead some with
the surveyors and engineers. Seems that I remember
you studied engineering yourself."

"For a while," Britten admitted. "I gave some
thought to going into that line of work. But then I ran
into you, sir."

Faraday grinned. "And you decided to become a
detective instead. Well, I'm glad of that." He opened a
drawer in his desk and took out a piece of paper.
Pushing it across the desk, he said, "Here's your
ticket. There's a westbound train leaving this evening,
and I've decided to put you on it. No point in waiting
any longer, is there?"

"No, sir," Britten replied with a shake of his head
and a smile. "I'll be ready to go."

"I've told Rowland when you will arrive, and he is
arranging for that draftsman's job to be waiting for
you when you get out to the railhead. You'll report to a

man named Terence Jennings. He's the head of construction."

"Does this Jennings know that I'm actually a detective?"

Faraday shook his head. "No one will know that. So
you'll be on your own out there, son. If there is a
traitor in the ranks, it could be anyone, anywhere. You
keep in touch, and anything I can do for you back
here, you just let me know."

"I will," Britten promised. "I'll send you a telegram
when I have some solid information, using our
standard code so I won't arouse anyone's suspicion."

"Good." Faraday's voice became more serious.
"Just be careful, Daniel. I don't know how much there
really is to Amos Rowland's hunch, but you could be
heading into trouble."

"I'll handle it," Britten said confidently.

Faraday stood up and extended his hand across the
desk. As Britten shook it, the older man said, "I know
you will."

Deep down, though, Britten had to admit that he
was a bit nervous about taking on a major assignment
like this on his own. He was less worried about his
safety, he realized, than he was about disappointing
Faraday and the agency.

As Britten turned toward the door, Faraday
stopped him by saying, "One more thing."

"Yes, sir?"

"What kind of gun do you have, Daniel?"

"A forty-four Starr, sir."

"Take it with you," Faraday advised.

When he was back in his rented room not far from
the rail yard, Britten spent an hour packing his clothes
in a small valise. After cleaning the Starr revolver, he
wrapped it in oilcloth and placed it in the valise as
well. Once he had arrived at the railhead, he would
arouse no suspicions by wearing the weapon—plenty
of men carried guns on the frontier—but displaying it
on the train itself might attract unwanted attention.

He also packed a set of draftsman's pens, which he had bought several years earlier when he was working with the surveyors on the Union Pacific, up in Nebraska. As he had told Faraday, he had been thinking at the time of going into engineering as a profession.

Britten smiled when he thought back to how he had become an investigative agent instead. Admiration for Matthew Faraday had played a part in it, but there had also been the lure of excitement, the challenge of an assignment just like the one he had now.

Once he was packed and ready to go, Britten spent the afternoon going over some of his books on railroading and engineering, most of them written by men who had gained their experience back east and had no idea of the obstacles facing frontier railroaders. Even so, Britten had studied those books to glean what he could from them. But he was more interested in the comparatively few studies that had been written about the Indians. A handful of white men such as Francis Parkman had traveled through the lands of the red man, living with the Indians, learning their ways, and returning to write about them. Britten was fascinated by their insights.

A part of him felt sorry for the Sioux and the Cheyenne. In the end they would lose their battle with the iron horse; of that he was sure. But he could almost admire their resistance, their determination to hang on to a way of life that was slowly vanishing.

But he had a job to do and a potential criminal to root out. After putting on his hat and slipping his pipe and tobacco pouch into his coat pocket, he lifted his valise and left his apartment. His step was light with anticipation early that evening as he walked toward the Kansas Pacific depot. According to the ticket in his pocket, the westbound train would pull out at five minutes after seven. Britten had plenty of time. The sun had gone down, but the western sky still had a faint tinge of pink in it.

He was passing through a section of warehouses not far from the tracks when a man came out of an alley

ahead of him. Britten hesitated as the man, wearing
the ragged clothes of a tramp, turned toward him. The
man tugged a greasy cap off his head as he stepped up
to Britten.

"Beg your pardon, mister," the stranger said in a
hoarse voice. "Would you be havin' the makin's for a
cigarette?"

Britten shook his head, relaxing somewhat. This
was a rough section of town, but it appeared that the
man just wanted to cadge a smoke. "Sorry," he said.
"I smoke a pipe."

The sudden scrape of a foot on the pavement
behind him was all the warning he had.

Instinctively, Britten flung himself to the side. He
heard the swish of air as something heavy passed close
by his head. Spinning around, he took several quick
steps backward while peering intently into the gloom
to see what he was facing.

Two more men had come up behind him, joining
the first one to present a united front. The man who
had asked for a cigarette held out his hand and rasped,
"We don't want trouble, mister. Just give us your
money."

The blood was pounding in Britten's head, although
strangely enough he did not feel particularly afraid.

He studied his opponents. The one in the middle,
the one who had spoken, was wiry and had narrow
shoulders. To his left was the one who had tried to
clout Britten from behind. Britten could see the
weapon now; it was a sock, probably filled with sand
or gravel. The third man was the biggest of the lot,
with a bushy dark beard.

Britten stood ready to move as they hesitated and
waited for his response. He said, "If I give you my
money, what happens then?"

The third man, the bearded one, answered, "You
still get a taste of my boot, you bastard."

That was the answer Britten had expected. They
wanted more than money. They wanted the excitement of beating up their victim. He wondered if he

could get the Starr out of his bag before they closed in on him.

Tired of waiting, the three toughs moved forward. The glow from a lamp down the street gave Britten a better look at the bearded man as he advanced. In that instant, Britten recognized him as Mose Goreham, a notorious local cutthroat. As part of his job, Britten tried to keep up with the criminals in the Kansas City area, and he knew that Goreham was one of the worst of the bunch, a man suspected of several killings. No one had ever been able to pin anything on him, however. That was because his victims always wound up dead, Britten suspected.

Britten glanced past his attackers, but he could not see anyone near enough to come to his aid. Several blocks down the street, people stood at the train station, but they were too far away to help, even if he could get their attention.

With a snarl, Goreham abruptly leaped toward him.

Britten jerked out of the way of the big man's lunge, but that brought him within range of the man with the makeshift blackjack. The weapon thudded into Britten's right shoulder, sending pain shooting through him. The valise slipped from his fingers.

The first man, seeing the bag on the ground, darted toward it, but Britten lashed out with his foot, kicking the valise into the alley. At that moment Goreham's hand closed on his left shoulder, yanking him around.

Britten saw the massive fist coming at him and ducked his head, driving forward inside the range of the blow. He straightened suddenly, and the top of his head caught Goreham in the face. Britten's hat cushioned the force of the blow to a certain extent before it fell to the ground, but the blow still rocked Goreham back on his heels. Britten sank his left fist in Goreham's belly.

His right arm numb for the moment, Britten pivoted to meet the charge of the second man as Goreham staggered away from him. This time Britten blocked the blow as the man swiped at him with the sock. The young agent brought his knee up, driving it into the attacker's groin, and taking a quick step back, he kicked again. Because the man had bent over to clutch the injured area, Britten's boot smacked into the side of his head, and the man flopped to the pavement of the street, out cold.

Britten spotted the other man, the one who had first approached him, in the alley searching for the valise. A few feet away, Goreham had recovered his balance and was ready to charge angrily toward him again. Britten considered his options at whirlwind speed and then launched himself into the alley.

Reaching out with his left hand, he caught the collar of the thug there and jerked him to one side, using the man's own momentum to run him into the wall of the warehouse on that side of the alley.

Behind him, Britten heard Goreham's pounding footsteps. He bent to scoop up the valise and yanked its catches open. With the feeling starting to come back into his right hand, he sent those fingers diving into the bag. They closed around the butt of the pistol through the oilcloth. It was unloaded, but Goreham had no way of knowing that.

Spinning around, Britten pulled the gun free and lined it on Goreham. The criminal stopped in his tracks.

Britten pulled back the Starr's hammer. "Just hold it," he said coldly. "You have a date with the law, my friend. You'll think twice before you try to rob another traveler."

Goreham's hands were slightly lifted, his eyes darting from side to side as he looked for cover. Obviously, none of them had expected this much resistance from Britten. The three robbers had probably underestimated him because of his size, and they had no way of knowing about the brawls he had been in, going all the way back to his keelboat days on the Mississippi.

A hand suddenly clawed at Britten's leg. The man he had run into the wall had hold of him. Britten swayed, almost falling, then slashed with the gun. Its barrel raked across the man's face, making him let go and roll away with a yelp of pain.

"Run!" Goreham snapped. "He's got a gun!"

The bearded tough turned and fled through the alley's mouth, pausing only to grab his unconscious comrade and drag him along. The third man scrabbled across the floor of the alley and then came up running.

Britten stood with the pistol leveled after them, but he did not fire. If they wondered why not, they did not slow down to worry about it, and within seconds they had vanished into the shadows.

Britten heaved a sigh. For a moment, he had been afraid that they would turn back on him when they realized he was not shooting. He picked up the valise and found the box of cartridges he had brought along for the Starr.

Quickly, he loaded five shells into the cylinder, leaving the sixth chamber empty for the hammer to rest on. He had heard that gunmen followed that practice, and it seemed like a sensible one. Then he slid the gun behind his belt.

Some of his clothes had spilled from the valise when he had removed the pistol, and among them he located a lightweight jacket, which would conceal the Starr to a certain extent. Shrugging into the jacket, he stuffed the other clothes back into the bag, and then he replaced his dust-covered hat on his head.

Pulling his watch from his pocket, Britten opened it and angled the face to catch what little light found its way into the mouth of the alley. He still had ten minutes to catch his train.

As he walked toward the depot, not wasting any time now, he considered what had just happened. There was a good chance that Goreham and his men had simply picked him as a likely-looking victim; such random robbery attempts were fairly common. But just in case there was more to it, he would let Matthew Faraday know what had occurred.

Britten brushed himself off as best he could, but as he entered the station he knew he still looked disheveled, since several travelers cast surprised glances at him. He went straight to the ticket window and asked the clerk on duty, "Is the westbound still on schedule?"

"You bet," the man answered, frowning at Britten from under his eyeshade. "She'll be pulling out in just a few minutes. Say, mister, you been wrestling wildcats or something?"

"Something," Britten answered shortly as he turned away from the window. The big clock on the station wall told him he still had four minutes. He sat down on one of the benches in the waiting room and pulled a pencil and a piece of paper from his pocket. Quickly, he scratched out a message giving the bare details of the attack on him by Mose Goreham and his confederates. Then he went back to the ticket window.

"Do you have an envelope?" he asked the clerk.

"Sure."

Britten took the envelope the man handed him and sealed the message inside it. "I need to get this to Matthew Faraday," he said. "Can you see that it reaches him?"

Faraday's name was well known. The clerk nodded and said, "I sure will, mister."

"Thanks. Now I've got to catch that train," Britten said. Outside on the platform the conductor was bellowing his all-aboard call.

"You got a ticket?" the clerk asked.

Britten patted his shirt pocket. Hefting the valise, he hurried through the doors to the platform. The steam whistle on the locomotive shrilled, and the wheels began to turn slowly.

Britten saw the conductor stepping onto the last passenger car. He waited until the steps came even with him, then stepped up himself, reaching out to grasp the railing with his free hand. The conductor was standing on the little platform at the rear of the car.

"You just made it, mister," he said. "Guess your luck's running good."

"I hope so," Britten replied. So far this evening, he did not feel very lucky, but he supposed it could have been a lot worse.

The conductor opened the door into the car and stepped aside to let Britten pass. As Britten entered the car, he scanned its occupants in the light of the swaying lanterns suspended from the ceiling. He saw farmers and drummers and businessmen, even a few plainly dressed women who were probably on their way to join husbands who had gone west ahead of them. Toward the front of the car was a knot of passengers who were more flashy than the others. The men were gamblers, judging from their clothes, and the two young women with them were definitely soiled doves.

It took all kinds on the frontier, Britten knew. As the train approached the railhead, the number of so-called respectable citizens would probably diminish. On the last leg of the trip, chances were that all of the passengers would be laborers, gamblers, or whores.

And, he thought, one detective.

Spotting an empty pair of seats about a quarter of the way up the coach, Britten moved toward them. He removed his hat, placing it and the valise on the aisle seat, and then took his place next to the window. Unobtrusively, he slipped the revolver into his bag, then took a deep breath and leaned back against the hard wooden seat. He pulled out his pipe and tobacco, filled the bowl, tamped it, and struck a match, drawing hard.

The train was picking up speed now, and there was a great clatter as it crossed the high bridge over the

Missouri River. Looking out, Britten could see a few lights reflecting on the muddy surface of the broad span of water.

"Why, Mr. Britten—or should I say Daniel?—I didn't expect to see you again so soon. What a pleasant surprise."

The familiar female voice made Britten jerk his head around. He stared up at the young woman standing in the aisle, one hand in a soft tan glove resting on the seatback to balance her. She wore a dark blue traveling outfit and a neat hat with a feather attached to it.

Britten realized she was waiting for a response to her greeting. He stood up quickly, glancing past her to see several porters loaded down with what had to be her baggage. He said, "Hello, Miss Rowland."

"Deborah," she reminded him.

"Deborah. I must admit I'm surprised to see you, as nice as it is. Might I inquire why you're here?"

"Probably the same reason as you, Daniel," Deborah replied, smiling sweetly. "I'm going to the railhead."

Chapter 4

AFTER A MOMENT BRITTEN RECOVERED FROM HIS SURPRISE upon seeing Deborah Rowland standing there. He reached over to remove his valise and hat from the empty seat and, standing, said to her, "I'd be pleased to have you join me."

The dark-haired woman laughed softly. "I would enjoy that, Daniel, but I'm afraid I have other accommodations waiting for me. The next car up is a private one, set aside for my father and members of his family. In this case, me."

"Oh."

Her head tilted to one side as she eyed his clothing with puzzlement. "Whatever happened to you?"

Britten looked down at himself in embarrassment. "Oh, I . . . I had a little run-in with some petty thieves—"

"My goodness, Daniel, I do hope you weren't hurt."

"No, I'm fine. Just a little the worse for wear." Britten glanced at the porters, who were waiting patiently with the heavy bags. "I'll let you pass on

51

through. It is certainly nice to see you again." He bowed slightly.

Abruptly, she reached out and took hold of his arm. "Come with me," she said. "I'd like for you to see the car."

Britten hesitated. "I'm not sure I should. After all, my seat is supposed to be back here—"

"Don't worry about that," Deborah interrupted. "As long as you're with me, no one is going to say anything about where you're sitting." She smiled. "Please. It's so good to see a familiar face. I thought I'd have to make the trip with no one for company."

Britten found himself unable to resist the imploring look she gave him. "All right." He told himself that it would not hurt to have a look at the private car she was obviously eager to show off. He could always come back here later and find another seat if this one had been taken.

Deborah slipped her arm through his and led the way up the aisle, the porters trailing behind them. Britten opened the door at the front of the car and held tightly to her arm as they negotiated the platforms between coaches. Cool night air tugged at the feather on Deborah's hat.

Britten had been in dozens of railroad cars before, but he had never seen one like the private coach into which Deborah Rowland led him. Most cars were constructed of the plainest wood available, inside and out, but this one was paneled with rich dark oak, though portions of the walls were covered with tastefully designed wallpaper. A warm light was cast by the two chandeliers suspended from the ceiling. Overstuffed armchairs were arranged around the room, centered by a large claw-footed sofa. Britten saw hinges on the back of the sofa, indicating that it could be opened into a good-sized bunk. At the far end of the coach was a stove, which could be used for cooking or heating or both, and beyond it was a small door. Britten had heard enough about these elaborate private cars to know that the door probably led into a washroom.

"Well," Deborah said, "what do you think, Daniel?"

"It's a far cry from the emigrant cars," Britten replied, setting his valise and hat near the wall.

"And I'm not an emigrant," Deborah said, sounding annoyed. "I'm not going to apologize for my father's wealth, Daniel. He worked hard to get where he is. He never let anything stand in his way."

"I'm sorry," Britten said quickly. "I meant no offense, Deborah. I'm just not accustomed to such elegance. Most of the trains I've ridden in the past have been work trains."

"You've been involved in railroad construction?"

"Oh, yes," Britten admitted. "In fact, that's why I'm here."

Deborah looked at him with curiosity as she removed her hat and flung it carelessly onto one of the chairs. She turned to the porters and said, "Put that baggage down carefully, please. My maid will unpack it later."

"Yes'm," the head porter said. He and his men placed the large valises in one corner of the car, then left through the rear door. Britten and Deborah were alone now.

She turned back to him. "You haven't asked why I'm going to the railhead."

Britten shrugged and said, "I didn't figure it was any of my business. I must admit I was a bit surprised by your destination. End-of-track is no place for a young lady of breeding."

"You sound like my father," Deborah said with a laugh. She sat down on the sofa and patted the cushion beside her. "He was positively livid when I told him I was making this journey."

Britten hesitated before sitting down beside her. He had brushed himself off as best he could following the attack by Mose Goreham and his thugs, but he was hardly as elegant as the young men who probably flocked around Deborah everywhere she went.

"Sit down," she insisted. "I won't bite you, Daniel."

Britten sat. "If your father objected to your trip, I'm surprised he didn't forbid it."

Deborah laughed again, and the merry sound touched something inside him. "Father knows better than to forbid me to do anything," she declared. "That only makes me want it all the more. Anyway, I don't see anything wrong with a woman going to the railhead."

"I imagine he was worried about your reputation. Most of the women out there are . . . uh . . . ladies of easy virtue."

"Prostitutes, you mean," Deborah said bluntly. "Now I've shocked you by being so plainspoken. That's a fault of mine, I'm afraid. But as I mentioned at my father's party, I intend to be running the Kansas Pacific someday, and I think I should learn everything about it that I can. Besides, I have another reason for going."

Britten wondered what that reason was, but Deborah said nothing else about it, and he put it out of his mind. He had other things to ponder. Deborah had not been forced to go through the car where he was sitting to reach this one. He suspected that she had known he was aboard and had sought him out.

Which could mean that she was interested in him, Britten reasoned. Interested enough to find out about his plans from her father, anyway. Had she found out anything else about him—that he was a detective, for instance?

She put a hand on his arm again and said, "You really are a godsend, Daniel. I had been prepared to spend my time reading during this trip, but now I have someone to talk to. I want you to take all of your meals with me, too."

Britten, feeling overwhelmed by her imperious attitude, took a deep breath and said, "Deborah, I should explain something to you. Your father offered me a job last night, and I accepted. I'm going to be working as a draftsman for the surveying crews at the railhead. I'm hardly proper company for a young lady such as yourself."

She frowned at him. "I thought you worked for Mr. Faraday."

Britten laughed, inwardly hoping she would accept the story he was concocting as he went along. "I was one of Mr. Faraday's clerks, nothing more. But he liked me and wanted me to meet your father, thinking that perhaps a better job would be available with the railroad. Luckily, it was."

"I see." Deborah gave a shake of her brunette head. "And I don't care. All this business of social classes is ridiculous, as far as I'm concerned. You're a sweet, handsome, intelligent young man, and I'd rather spend my time with you than with any of those rich dullards back in Kansas City." Her smile was dazzling. "What do you think of that, Mr. Daniel Britten?"

Britten had to smile back at her. "I think I know when I'm beaten," he chuckled. "I'll be more than happy to be your . . . traveling companion, Miss Rowland."

She moved closer to him, and he could feel the warmth of her body through their clothes. She squeezed his arm. "Good. I'm glad that's settled. Have you had dinner?"

Britten shook his head. "As a matter of fact, I haven't. I was going to try to buy something at our next stop."

Deborah made a face and said, "You don't want to do that. The food at those stops is awful. That's something that I shall certainly improve once I'm in charge. I'll have Alice prepare something."

"Alice?"

"My maid. She should be here shortly. She's talking to the conductor right now about the special requirements for my journey."

Britten nodded. He was not surprised that Deborah was traveling with a servant. Talking about social equality was easy to do; practical considerations were another matter.

He was sure of one thing—with Deborah Rowland on board the train, this journey to end-of-track was certainly going to be more interesting than he had expected.

The meal prepared by Deborah's stout, middle-aged maid was excellent, and that came as a surprise to Britten. Working only with the heavy iron stove in the front corner of the private car, Alice managed to cook ham and sweet potatoes and a loaf of light, fluffy bread. Britten thoroughly enjoyed the food, and he had to admit that Deborah made a charming dinner companion. She was opinionated, to be sure, but she also displayed a higher degree of education than was usual for a woman.

Evidently she meant what she said about someday being in charge of the railroad and wanting to be well prepared.

After dinner Alice served brandy, pouring it from an elegant cut-glass decanter. Deborah surprised Britten by taking a snifter for herself—he had never known a lady who drank hard liquor.

"Have you ever been to a railhead?" he asked as they sipped their drinks.

"Well . . . no," Deborah admitted. "But I've heard a great deal about them. According to my father, there's no more sinful place on earth."

"I'm afraid he's right."

Deborah gave him another of those innocent but somehow mischievous smiles and said, "It seems to me that every young lady needs a little education in the ways of sin. At least that way she knows what she's missing."

To that, Britten made no reply.

A short while later he stood up and reached for his

hat. "I'd better be getting back to the other car," he said. "I want a place to sit tonight."

"It won't be easy sleeping in one of those hard seats," Deborah commented.

"Perhaps not, but it's better than standing up."

Deborah shrugged. "I suppose so." She started to say something else, then stopped. Finally, she went on. "Good night, Daniel. Will you join me for breakfast in the morning?"

Britten considered for a moment, then nodded. He did not see what harm it could do. "I'd be happy to," he said, picking up his valise. "Good night."

She was still smiling at him as he stepped out onto the platform at the rear of the car and closed the door behind him. He paused for a moment and leaned on the railing around the platform, watching the shadow-covered plains rolling by.

For the most part the prairie was dark. Occasionally a small light could be seen here and there, a lantern burning in some lonely farmer's soddy. Overhead the stars were brilliant and glittering, and a three-quarter moon turned silver the several wisps of cloud drifting in front of it. It was a beautiful land in its own harsh way, Britten thought.

Despite his having enjoyed the evening with Deborah, he wished she had not picked this train for her journey to the railhead. He wished she were not going there at all. Deborah Rowland was beautiful and charming and a distraction he did not need. Also, he knew that if any trouble arose, he was going to feel compelled to protect her.

There was not a damned thing he could do about the situation, though. A lowly draftsman could not request that the daughter of a major stockholder in the road be put off the train and sent back to Kansas City. He would just have to make the best of it.

Over the next hours and days, Britten managed to do just that. As Deborah had decreed, he took all his meals with her, and when he saw some of the dining rooms at the stations where the train stopped, he was glad. The train passed through Topeka, then traveled on to the rude hamlet called Abilene. Britten had never seen such a miserable collection of shacks and shanties, but he heard talk during the stopover that men from Texas were planning to bring their herds of longhorn cattle north to Kansas. If that happened, all the little towns through which the rails passed would soon be booming, Britten thought. There was a hungry market for beef back east.

On the train rolled to Fort Ellsworth. Beyond this point there were few settlements, and his prediction as to the kinds of passengers who would be aboard the train proved to be true. Anyone still on board was bound for end-of-track and whatever hell-on-wheels town was there.

So far the passengers aboard the train had seen no Indians, although Britten had kept an eye out for them through the windows of Deborah's private car. Whenever he brought up the subject, she waved off the threat. "Those savages simply like to put on a show," she declared. "They know better than to really bother us."

Britten thought that such a statement proved how little Deborah Rowland knew about the Sioux and the Cheyenne, who were deadly serious in their opposition to the iron horse.

The train was expected to reach the railhead early in the evening. During the middle of the afternoon before its arrival, while Britten and Deborah were in her car and engaging in a spirited discussion of the War Between the States and its destructive aftermath, there was a sudden shrill blast from the train's whistle. A moment later, the train ground its brakes and lurched to a halt.

Britten sat up straight, sensing trouble. Deborah lost her air of languor and turned toward the windows. "What is it?" she asked excitedly.

Rising, he stepped to the window and leaned over to peer through the glass. He was familiar with what he was seeing, but even so he found the awesomeness of it hard to accept. "Buffalo," he said simply.

Standing beside him at the window, Deborah caught her breath as she looked out at a shaggy sea of brown. The herd of buffalo extended as far as the eye could see to the north of the tracks. Britten turned to the windows on the other side of the coach and saw that the herd must have just started across the tracks. Only a few dozen of the animals were on that side of the train, but thousands were waiting to cross.

The whistle was still blowing, and gunfire erupted from the other cars. Judging from the whoops of laughter that blended with the other sounds, the passengers were enjoying themselves.

"I've never seen anything so . . . so . . . magnificent," Deborah said in awe.

"You won't see such things for many more years, the way the buffalo are being slaughtered," Britten replied.

"Oh, surely you can't mean that," Deborah protested. "Just because some of the men on the trains take potshots at them—"

"Men who make their living hunting buffalo sometimes kill a thousand in a day," Britten said flatly. "They kill the animals to feed the laborers at the railhead and also to help feed the army troops stationed around here. Sooner or later the buffalo will be wiped out. And that'll be the end of the Indians as well."

"What's so bad about that?"

Britten just shook his head and made no reply. Deborah came from a different world; through no fault of her own, she would never understand, no matter how hard he tried to explain it.

Ignoring his silence, Deborah went on. "I want a closer look at those beasts. Let's go out on the platform."

She did not wait for Britten's reply, and he could do nothing except trail after her as she quickly opened the rear door and stepped out.

The buffalo crowded against the train, mere feet from where Deborah stood clutching the railing, her lovely features flushed with excitement. She wrinkled her nose and grinned at Britten. "They have quite an odor, don't they?" she asked.

"I've heard tell that a man never forgets it once he's smelled it," Britten replied. He stood close beside her, ready to grab her if she should lose her grip. Evidently she did not realize the grisly fate that would be in store for her should she fall into the mass of creatures.

More guns cracked from the other cars. Leaning out slightly, Britten could see men hanging from open windows and firing handguns and rifles into the herd, some of them foolishly climbing onto the tops of the cars. The shriek of the whistle again split the afternoon air.

"Do you have a gun, Daniel?" Deborah asked, her hand on his arm. "I want to try to shoot one of them."

Britten faced her levelly. "Why?"

The question seemed to take her by surprise. "Why —all those other people are. I just assumed that I would have the same right."

"What good would it do you to kill a buffalo?" Britten heard the anger creeping into his voice, but he could do nothing to stop it. "A dead buffalo will feed an Indian family for a week, and then they'll use practically every bit of its carcass for other purposes. The hide will make a blanket to keep a baby warm, or clothes for a squaw, or a tepee to shelter the whole family." His tone was scathing as he went on. "You shoot a buffalo, Deborah, and it won't do a damned thing but lie there and rot."

She stared at him for a second, stunned by his anger, and then her own face flushed. "You can't talk to me that way!" she snapped. Her hand flashed toward his face, but his fingers caught her wrist, stopping the slap in midair.

"It's the truth," he grated, and as he gripped her wrist tightly, he felt a shudder run through her. He was almost as surprised by his vehemence as she was; he had not known that he felt as strongly about the matter as he did.

Deborah caught her bottom lip between white teeth. "I . . . I'm sorry," she said. "I didn't understand, Daniel."

Britten started to release her hand, but he stopped abruptly, maintaining his grip, and then he truly surprised both of them: He drew her closer to him and kissed her.

Oblivious to the whistling of the train, the gunfire from the coach windows, and the rumble of the passing herd, Britten kissed her long and hard. For a moment she resisted, but then she relaxed in his embrace, returning the kiss with a warmth and sweetness that set his head spinning. When she finally pulled away from him, they were both breathless.

His fingers twined with hers, and for a time they stood watching the buffalo, saying nothing, while up in the cab of the train the drivers waited impatiently until they could get their locomotive going again. After a while, she rested her head against his shoulder.

The delay stretched late into the afternoon, but Britten and Deborah did not care.

The memory of that kiss lingered in Britten's mind through the rest of the afternoon. The locomotive was finally able to inch its way through the buffalo herd, but the delay meant that the train would be arriving at the railhead sometime in the hours before dawn.

As the train picked up speed again, Britten and Deborah went back into her car. Moments later the conductor appeared with a knock on the door, and as Britten admitted him, the man touched the brim of his cap and said, "Beg your pardon, Miss Rowland, but while we were stopped back there some of the boys managed to get some buffalo steaks. I was wondering if you'd like a couple for dinner this evening."

Deborah hesitated, glancing at Britten, who sensed that she was waiting for his approval. He nodded and said, "Buffalo steaks are tasty, all right."

Deborah turned back to the conductor. "That would be fine, thank you."

The man tugged his cap again. "I'll bring some."

Deborah left the preparation of the steaks to Alice, who outdid herself as far as Britten was concerned. While the train raced over the prairie and night fell, Britten and Deborah enjoyed the meal, sitting on opposite sides of the table, which folded out from the wall of the private car. Covered by a spotless white linen cloth, the table was lit by a pair of candles in ornately engraved gilt holders. Deborah had ordered the lamps in the chandeliers extinguished.

When the meal was done and Alice had withdrawn, leaving Deborah and Britten alone, the young woman leaned back in her chair, sipping delicately from the snifter of brandy she held. "Have you enjoyed this journey, Daniel?" she asked with a smile.

"You know I have," he replied, drinking from his own glass. "I was prepared for a rather boring trip to the railhead."

"How would you have passed your time if I hadn't shown up? Would you have joined that card game in the next car? Alice says it never breaks up."

Britten shook his head. "Poker's not my game."

There were little fires dancing in Deborah's eyes as she said, "Then you would have no doubt spent some time with those painted ladies. I hear they're doing business as usual."

"That's not my game, either," Britten said with a laugh.

Deborah took a bigger swallow of her brandy. "What *is* your game, Daniel Britten?"

"I like to read—" he began.

Deborah placed the snifter on the table and stood up. She came around the table and rested her hand on his shoulder. In a whisper, she said, "I mean, what do you do for fun?" She knelt, putting her face level with his. "This?"

As her mouth brazenly found his, Britten's arms reached out of their own volition and went around her. Slowly he rose, drawing her with him, though his lips did not leave hers. Her body pressed hotly to his.

Daniel Britten had always considered himself an honorable man, but he was also quite human, and there was no denying the attraction he felt for Deborah. She was a lovely, intelligent young woman—and evidently she wanted him as badly as he wanted her.

Somehow the two of them wound up standing beside the sofa. Deborah rested her face against his chest and, without looking up at him, said, "It makes a fine bed, Daniel."

"I'm sure it does," he murmured as his hands caressed her shoulders and slid down her back. She made a soft sound of contentment in her throat.

There was no turning back now, and both of them knew it.

Afterward Britten was unsure just exactly who had done the seducing. Deborah was more open in her desires than most women, and he was certain that she had enjoyed the lovemaking every bit as much as he had. Yet as he rested his weight on an elbow and looked down at her lying beside him, he felt compelled to apologize.

He stroked her cheek with his fingertips, causing her to snuggle closer to him. "Deborah," he began, "I want you to know that even though we haven't known each other for very long, you mean a great deal to me already. I want to apologize for taking advantage of you—"

He broke off as she shook her head and gave a merry little laugh. "Don't be ridiculous, Daniel," she said.

She rested a hand on his bare chest. "What happened tonight was something we both wanted."

He opened his mouth to speak, but she stopped him with a finger on his lips.

Her arms went around him, drawing him down to her as she whispered into his ear, "I don't know about you, but I want it *again. . . .*"

Chapter 5

LATER, WITH DEBORAH STILL IN HIS ARMS, BRITTEN DOZED again. He was not sure how much time had passed when the shrill whistle of the train penetrated his slumber. He lifted his head, shook it groggily for a moment, then swung his legs off the bed.

Deborah reached out for him, her hands warm on his bare flesh. "Stay," she murmured.

"Sorry," Britten told her, patting a flank covered by a silk sheet. He stood up and moved to one of the windows, pulling aside the canvas curtain covering it. Shading his eyes with a hand, he peered out into the night.

Back to the east the faintest tinge of pink colored the sky. Dawn was not too far away, and that meant the railhead was close, too. Britten swung away from the window and bent to pick up his clothes.

Through sleepy, slitted eyes, Deborah watched him for a moment and then said, "You know you don't have to leave, Daniel."

"You have a reputation to protect, Deborah. I don't want to compromise it."

"Do you honestly think that Alice doesn't know what went on tonight?" she asked.

"There's a chance she doesn't. I'd like to keep it that way, for your sake."

Deborah gave a throaty laugh. "If I'm not worried about my reputation, why should you be?"

"Because I'm supposed to be," Britten replied with a frown as he shrugged into his shirt.

"You feel guilty, don't you? Daniel, what went on between us was my idea."

Without looking at her, he said, "I want you to know that I'll marry you, if that's what you'd like."

Deborah laughed even louder at that. "Did I even bring up matrimony, Daniel?"

"Well, no . . ." Britten's frown deepened.

"And I'm not going to." She flung back the cover and rose from the bed, ignoring her nudity as she walked toward him. Resting her hands on his chest, she went on. "You're a gentleman. I know that, and I'm not trying to make fun of you. But I have no intention of marrying you, Daniel—no matter how sweet and kind you are."

Britten's face was taut as he nodded. "I understand."

Deborah clucked her tongue. "Now you think I'm some sort of wanton woman, don't you? I'm not. I just don't believe in false, ridiculous standards." She leaned against him, lifting her face, finding his mouth with hers. Britten could not stop his arms from going around her. When she broke the kiss, she put her face against his chest and murmured, "Marriage to you might not be so bad. But it's absolutely impossible, Daniel."

This time when he said, "I understand," his voice was softer, more compassionate. He did understand. The two of them came from different worlds, and her father would never allow such a marriage. As for himself, he was a detective with a job to do.

She slipped out of his embrace, and he let her go.

Her nudity had been having a pronounced effect on him, and there was no time for more lovemaking. If he did not get out of that car soon, he would never be able to leave before the train reached end-of-track.

"I'm going back to the other car," he said as he finished dressing. "I'm sure I'll be seeing you around the railhead. How long will you be staying?"

Deborah picked up a dressing gown and slid her arms into it. As she belted it around her slim waist, she said, "I'm not sure. But you sound like this is good-bye, Daniel."

"Isn't it? We can't continue our involvement in this manner once we're at the railhead."

"I suppose you're right, but that doesn't mean I have to like it." Deborah came to him as he picked up his valise, and then she kissed him lightly. "Good-bye, Daniel."

Not trusting himself to say anything, Britten slipped one arm around her and hugged her tightly for a moment, then released her and turned to the door of the coach. He went out without looking back.

As he stood on the platform between the cars, he paused. By leaning out slightly, he could see the lights of the railhead, now less than a mile away. They would be at end-of-track within minutes. Britten saw no point in taking a seat in one of the regular passenger cars, deciding instead to wait there on the platform. As far as anyone at the railhead was concerned, he was simply eager to arrive.

As the train's brakes began to squeal, Britten looked out on the prairie, where he could see tents scattered on both sides of the tracks. Most of the smaller tents, used for sleeping, were dark at this hour, but the big ones were still ablaze with light; though the large structures were temporary, they were saloons, nevertheless, and as such never closed. A few wooden structures stood here and there, including several sheds where construction equipment was stored, and the station itself, which was a rather flimsy-looking

building. The tracks ran on past the makeshift settlement, disappearing into the night, but Britten knew
they ran out within a mile or so.

As the train shuddered to a stop, he hefted his valise
and stepped down onto the station platform. Several
men were there, obviously waiting for the train.
Among them was one who stood out from the others.
He was tall and wide-shouldered and carried himself
with an air of authority, even though he was dressed in
boots, work pants, and a coarse shirt like his companions.

The man came toward Britten and gave him a
friendly nod before bounding up the steps onto the
platform at the front of Deborah's private car. In the
light of the lanterns that hung from the awning over
the station platform, Britten saw that the man had a
broad, open face and a thatch of mud-colored hair
under his broad-brimmed hat. The muscles of his
shoulders bulged against his shirt as he lifted a hand
and knocked on the door of Deborah's car.

"Deborah! It's me, darlin'!" he called in a deep
voice.

Britten frowned and moved down the platform,
carrying his valise. The other cars were being unloaded now, the laborers, gamblers, and prostitutes
glad finally to have reached their destination. Britten
turned toward the crude frame station building at one
end of the platform, intending to ask for directions to
the construction boss's quarters. It was pretty early in
the morning to be reporting for work, but the camp
seemed to be waking up anyway.

A glad female cry made him pause and look back.
Deborah had emerged from her car, resplendent in a
pink frock, her hair gleaming and a smile on her face.
From her appearance no one would have believed that
less than fifteen minutes earlier she had been nude
and snuggled in his arms in her bed. He watched as
she threw herself into the arms of the tall, brawny man
who had pounded on her door, and his mouth came
down on hers in a long, hungry kiss.

Now Britten understood why she had said she could not marry him.

The man holding her peered down at her and said, "You look better than ever, sweetheart." With an arm still around her, he turned to the other men who had been standing with him on the platform. "Unload Miss Rowland's bags, will you, boys?" There was an easy tone of command in his voice.

The workers hurried to do as they were told, while Deborah and the man stepped down onto the station platform. Britten wondered who he was, feeling sure that he was someone important around there.

Britten had just started to turn away again when Deborah's voice stopped him. "Daniel!" she called. "Daniel Britten!"

When he looked back, she was waving to him, summoning him over to them. Britten took a deep breath. It was hard enough realizing that to Deborah he had been little more than a way to pass the time on a boring journey; now he was going to be painfully reminded of it.

Nevertheless, he could not bring himself to be rude to her, and he shouldered his way through the press of people across the platform.

When he reached the place where Deborah and the tall man were standing, Deborah reached out, that dazzling smile still on her lovely face, and rested a hand on his arm. "I'm glad you didn't get away, Daniel," she said brightly. "I want you to meet someone. Daniel Britten, this is Terence Jennings."

The name was familiar to Britten. As Jennings extended a big hand, Britten realized that he was the construction boss, the very man to whom Britten was to report.

"Glad to meet you, Britten," Jennings said heartily. "You're the new draftsman Mr. Rowland wired me to expect, aren't you?"

Britten shook hands with him, feeling the power in Jennings's grip. "That's right," he said.

"He's more than that," Deborah declared. "He's

my friend, Terence. He kept me company on the trip out here."

"Well, thank you for that, Britten. I was worried enough about Deborah coming out here. I'm glad there was someone along to keep an eye on her." A grin spread across Jennings's face. "You know how these women are; once they get an idea in their heads, there's no dealing with them."

"I wouldn't say that," Britten commented, and as he saw the lights dancing in Deborah's eyes, he wondered just what kind of a game she was playing.

"I couldn't help it," she said with a mock pout. "No girl wants to spend months at a time away from the man she's going to marry. As I told you, Daniel, I want to learn as much about this railroad as I can, but I suppose you could say that Terence is the real reason I came out here."

Britten's mouth tightened slightly, and he had to struggle to hide his embarrassment as he stood there with the smiling couple. She was as brazen a woman as he had ever encountered. If Jennings knew what had really gone on just hours earlier . . .

Britten, noticing the Navy Colt holstered on the other man's right hip, thought that Jennings might well try to use the gun if he knew the truth. Surely Deborah had the sense to keep quiet about it.

Jennings clapped a hand on Britten's shoulder. "I reckon you're anxious to get to work. Why don't you give me a chance to get the lady settled in, and then come over to my office in about half an hour? It's that tent right over there." He indicated a good-sized tent about thirty yards from the station. "I'll show you around and introduce you to the men you'll be working with."

"Sounds fine." Britten touched the brim of his hat and inclined his head toward Deborah. "Good morning, Miss Rowland. I hope you enjoy your stay."

"I'm sure I will," she said. "In fact, I already am."

Britten watched as Jennings led her down the steps at one end of the station platform and toward another tent not far from his. Behind them trailed the men carrying her baggage.

The sky had lightened considerably by now, and from the red glow on the horizon Britten knew that the sun would soon be up. Despite the early hour the construction camp was bustling with activity, and men were hurrying everywhere. On a nearby siding the locomotive of a work train was getting up steam. Shortly it would pull out for the actual railhead, bearing its load of ties, rails, and the men to put them down.

Since Britten had a few minutes to spare, he decided to take a look around. At first glance this camp was little different from others he had seen. After climbing down the steps of the platform, he turned toward what passed for a main street: a dusty artery that ran between several of the largest tent saloons.

As he walked past one of the brightly lit tents, he wondered just how much Terence Jennings actually knew about Deborah. Britten had felt an instinctive liking for the man. As the head of a railroad construction camp, Jennings had to be many things: engineer, surveyor, tracklayer, and brawler. His strength was probably as important to his job as his mind was, since he had to keep the rough-and-tumble workers in line and get the most out of them that he could. Such a man seemed an unlikely marriage partner for a young woman of wealth and breeding like Deborah, but he was clearly in love with her.

And despite everything that had happened, Britten could not bring himself to dislike Deborah. What had passed between them had been a special experience, and Britten knew he would never forget it, even though he had to put it behind him now.

As he walked down the dusty road mulling over these recent events, his thoughts were interrupted by a sudden pounding of hoofbeats and a hoarse yell. "Watch it there, sonny!" someone shouted from the back of a horse that was suddenly almost on top of him.

Britten jerked aside to let the animal thunder past him, but in doing so his feet tangled together, and his balance deserted him. He sat down hard in the street, raising a puff of dust.

The man on horseback reined in his mount and wheeled it around. He looked down at Britten and asked, "You all right, little feller?"

Britten stared up at the rider, a thick-bodied man with shoulders about as wide as Terence Jennings's. He had a drooping mustache that was shot through with gray, as was the thick dark hair under his pushed-back hat. He wore a buckskin jacket and pants, with fringe on the sleeves and down the legs. Protruding from the top of one high black boot was the hilt of a Bowie knife, and strapped around his waist was a Colt Dragoon. There was a rifle in the man's saddle boot, but Britten could not tell what kind it was.

The impudent smile on the man's face, coupled with the term "little feller" and everything else that had happened in the last hour, was simply too much for Britten. His temper finally boiling over, he surged to his feet and snapped, "Why the hell don't you watch where you're going, you old buffalo?"

The man in buckskins frowned. "Who you callin' old, sonny?" He swung one leg over the back of his horse and dropped from the saddle with a grace unusual in a man of his size. "I was on my way somewheres, but I reckon I could stop long enough to teach you a few manners."

Britten's fists clenched. "Go ahead," he said, and then the rational part of his brain shouted a warning at him. What the hell was he doing? This old-timer was big enough to tear him in half.

The man let out a booming laugh. "Wouldn't hardly be fair now, would it?" he asked. "And nobody can say that Sam Callaghan don't fight fair."

Britten realized that the big man was giving him a way out, but he found himself unable to take it.

Stepping forward, he said, "It's fair enough. You may be big, but you're an old man."

The grin fell from Sam Callaghan's face. "Don't like bein' called old," he rumbled. "Reckon I've seen a lot more winters than you, boy, but that don't mean I can't whip you." He handed his horse's reins to one of the men in the crowd that was rapidly gathering around them. "If you're such a damned fool that you're bound an' determined to try, reckon I got to oblige."

Britten nodded and shrugged out of his jacket. He knew he was probably going to regret this, but backing down now was something he could not do.

He tensed as Sam Callaghan moved slowly toward him, spat on his hands, and rubbed them together. As Callaghan tilted his head and glared at Britten with squinty eyes, a growl rose in his throat, and Britten wondered just how bad a beating he had let himself in for.

"Callaghan!"

The angry shout made both men freeze. Terence Jennings came pushing through the crowd around them, his face flushed.

"What're you buttin' in for, Jennings?" Callaghan snapped.

Jennings came to a stop in front of the big, buckskinned man and snarled, "I've warned you about brawling, Callaghan. I'm tired of you picking fights with every other man in camp."

"Didn't start this one," Callaghan rumbled. "This little feller, here, got feisty."

Britten stepped forward. "I don't like being called little, Callaghan, any more than you like being called old."

Callaghan cast a wide eye toward him. "Difference bein' that I ain't old and you are a sawed-off runt."

"That's enough!" Jennings stepped between the two men. "Move along, Callaghan. That's an order."

Callaghan scowled at the construction boss for

several moments, then gave a shrug. "All I wanted in the first place was to get on 'bout my business." He looked past Jennings's shoulder and said to Britten, "Reckon I'll see you again, sonny."

"That's fine with me," Britten said flatly.

Callaghan wheeled around, took the reins of his horse back from the bystander who was holding them, and climbed into the saddle. He kicked the horse into motion, and as the crowd scattered, the big man galloped away down the street, heading toward end-of-track.

Britten took a deep breath as Jennings turned toward him. The construction boss had a stern look on his face, but the hint of a grin played around the corners of his mouth. "Was that true, Britten?" he asked. "Did you call the tune on that dance?"

Britten laughed humorlessly. "I'm afraid I did. Not very smart, right?"

"You could say that. Callaghan's an old curly wolf. He's probably been in more brawls than you and I put together, and he fights to win, no holds barred. If he doesn't like you, you'd do well to steer clear of him."

Britten shrugged. "I don't like running."

"I need good draftsmen," Jennings said seriously. "You can't do the Kansas Pacific any good if you're hurt."

Britten nodded slowly. "I guess you're right." He glanced around; there was no sign of Deborah. "Where's Miss Rowland?"

"I believe she and her maid are unpacking in her tent. I was just in the way, what with all that feminine frippery being thrown around, so I decided to come hunt you up. I'm glad I did."

"Me, too," Britten admitted with a slight smile.

"Come on. I'll introduce you to Osgood Newton. He's our chief draftsman."

Britten fell in beside Jennings as the construction boss started down the street. The crowd had broken up, everyone going back to his own business, and the sun now flooded the plains with a reddish-gold light.

"What's Callaghan's job around here?" Britten asked after a moment.

"He's one of our scouts," Jennings replied. "He works with the surveying crews, helping them to chart our route, and he also furnishes some protection for them in case of Indian attack. He does a little buffalo hunting for us, too."

"He certainly is pugnacious."

"He's a blasted troublemaker!" Jennings snorted. "He seems to think we're doing a bad thing by building this railroad, even though it pays his salary. Like a lot of those old mountain men, he lived with the Indians for a while, and to hear him tell it, they're doing the right thing by trying to stop us. Not only that, but he thinks we mistreat the workers. We don't pay them enough, we work them too hard—Callaghan's got a complaint about everything. He's a man with some strange ideas, Britten, and like I said, he's a good man to steer clear of."

"I'll remember that." Britten nodded, thinking that he would remember everything about Sam Callaghan. Jennings's words had aroused his suspicions, and Britten wondered with which tribe Callaghan had lived. The scout was just the type of man who might be able to keep the Indians stirred up and causing trouble, and he had easy access to information about the railroad's progress that he could pass on to them.

It was something to think about, all right.

Jennings pushed back the canvas flap over a tent opening and called, "Visitors, Osgood. Are you up?"

"Of course," came the reply. "Come in, Mr. Jennings."

Jennings stepped into the tent, Britten following behind him. Along one canvas wall was a narrow cot, but most of the room in the tent was taken up by a large table. Several rolls of paper, which Britten recognized as large-scale maps, rested on one end of the table. One of the maps had been unrolled, and the man sitting at the table was making notations on it.

The draftsman was a spare man with a fringe of white hair around his ears and bushy white eyebrows. Other than that, his head was bald. He had a large, beaked nose and clear, intense blue eyes, which glanced up at Jennings and Britten as he said in a dry voice, "Good morning. I should have this map finished in just a little while, Mr. Jennings."

"Let me guess," Jennings grunted. "You were up before dawn, working by lanternlight again. That's not good for your eyes, Osgood."

"Nothing's wrong with my eyes," the man said distantly, his attention back on his work.

"Well, I've brought you some more help anyway. This is our new draftsman, Daniel Britten. Daniel, Osgood Newton."

Britten stepped forward. "I'm pleased to meet you, sir, and I'm eager to begin working with you."

Newton looked up at him for perhaps a second. "Hello."

Jennings put a hand on Britten's shoulder and said, "Osgood's sort of caught up in his work. But that's what makes him good at it, I suppose."

"You just tell me what you want done, Mr. Newton, and I'll be glad to do it," Britten said.

"Coffee," Newton replied curtly. "There's a dining hall a few tents over. Bring me some coffee."

Britten glanced at Jennings and saw the construction boss's shrug and half smile. Evidently Osgood Newton was a pretty acerbic individual.

"All right," Britten said. "I suppose you want it black?"

"How else?"

"Well, I'll leave you two to get acquainted," Jennings said heartily. "You're in good hands, Britten."

The construction boss ducked out of the tent before Britten could say anything else. For a moment, Britten stood there, unsure of how to proceed.

"I thought you were going to get coffee for us," Newton spoke up, his gaze still directed toward the map.

Britten decided to point out that he was a draftsman, too. "Mr. Osgood," he said, "with all due respect, I have to tell you that I didn't come all this way just to fetch coffee."

At the sharp tone in Britten's voice, Newton looked up, put his pen down, and pushed the inkwell aside. "Is that so?" he asked.

"Yes, sir, I'm afraid it is."

Newton grunted. "Good. Because there's a damned lot of work to do in building a railroad. We're going to push those rails clear across this country, and you'll do your share or I'll kick you all the way back to Kansas City. Understand?"

Britten stiffened, then saw the hint of humor around Newton's mouth. The man was going to be a hard taskmaster, but Britten suddenly had a feeling that Osgood Newton was damned good at his job.

Britten nodded. "I understand," he said.

Chapter 6

As soon as Britten returned with the coffee, Newton had work ready for him that was better suited to his assumed identity. He was to copy one of the maps that Newton had prepared, and he found himself enjoying the work, painstaking though it was.

The next couple of days were busy ones. From the looks of things, Newton had been sorely in need of an assistant. Quite a bit of work was waiting to be done, and Britten threw himself into the chore, proving quite capable at everything Newton gave him to do. They worked long hours, sitting on opposite sides of the big table, and at night Britten was content to go directly back to the tent to which he had been assigned and fall asleep on the cot.

So far there had been no trouble, but neither had Britten been able to do any investigating, since Newton was keeping him too busy. Maybe a draftsman was not the best choice for a cover identity.

By the morning of the third day several more miles of track had been laid and almost the entire camp picked up and moved. After the tents were struck, they were loaded on one of the work trains along with men and equipment and hauled to end-of-track. Even some of the frame buildings were knocked apart and transported to the new railhead, though others were left behind, including the depot. Maybe a town would grow up in the spot being left behind; only time would tell.

Britten's duties as a draftsman were put aside as he helped in the move. By the end of the day, most of the tents were back up in the new location, and work was under way on a new station.

Britten, being practically chained to his work as he had been, had not seen Deborah since the morning of their arrival. But as the hubbub in the new camp began to settle down somewhat that evening, he strolled down the rude street and found himself in front of Jennings's tent. The flap opened as he walked past, and Deborah and Jennings stepped out.

"Daniel!" Deborah exclaimed. "Where have you been hiding yourself?"

Britten took off his hat and nodded a greeting to the couple. "I've been a little busy," he said.

"I imagine Osgood has kept you hopping," Jennings said.

"We should be caught up with the work in a day or so," Britten commented. He thought Deborah looked especially lovely tonight in a brown dress that matched her hair. A silver pendant—a present from Jennings, no doubt—hung from a chain around her neck.

"Why don't you have dinner with us tonight?" Deborah asked. "Alice is still cooking for me, and I'm sure her fare is better than what you'd get in that dining hall."

"Yes," Jennings said before Britten had a chance to reply. "Please, join us."

Britten hesitated. He sensed that Jennings would prefer to eat alone with Deborah and was just being polite by extending the invitation. Besides, eating in the dining hall with the other workers always gave Britten a chance to listen to their conversation, a valuable practice since their gossip and complaints might yield information useful to his investigation. So far that was the only form of investigation he had been able to employ.

"I'm sorry," he said. "I've already promised to eat with Mr. Newton and some of the surveyors. We're going to be discussing the route."

That was true enough; he knew that Newton planned to talk to the surveyors, and he thought the chief draftsman would not mind his joining them.

Jennings nodded and said, "I understand. You seem to be fitting right in, Britten."

"I hope so. I enjoy the work."

"Newton will be sending you out with one of the surveying crews before long, I'd wager."

Britten hoped that was true. He was eager to get away from the camp and get a look at the terrain.

Deborah had a disappointed look on her face. "I don't see why you men have to talk business all the time," she said. "But I guess I'll just have to be satisfied with your promise that you'll dine with us some other time, Daniel."

"You have it," he said solemnly.

Britten was about to say good evening to them when the sudden braying of a mule made him turn around. He heard laughter from some of the other men in the camp, and then he saw a strange sight coming down the street toward them.

It was a wagon being pulled by a pair of mules. The sideboards were covered with pegs, and on the pegs hung pots, pans, harnesses, tools, and just about anything that anyone would need on the frontier. The whole thing gave off a clangor as the items swung against one another. The bed of the wagon was covered with a tattered piece of canvas flung over a rickety framework, and the gaping holes in the cover revealed that the wagon was stacked full of all sorts of goods, from sugar and flour to boxes containing ladies' hats.

On the seat of the wagon were two people. The one holding the reins of the team was an old man in a chewed-up buffalo coat, his cheek bulging with a massive chaw of tobacco. His hatless head was bald and shiny except for tufts of white hair sticking out above his ears. In a way, he reminded Britten of Osgood Newton, but unlike the chief surveyor, this individual was fat and incredibly dirty, the grime on his face appearing to be a permanent part of his skin.

Sitting beside him was a young woman. Judging from her slender shape, she was little more than a girl, really, Britten thought, although he could not get a good look at her. Her face was downcast, and she sat with her shoulders slumped in an air of dejection and despair. She wore a simple cotton dress that was heavily patched, and on her head was perched a battered, shapeless felt hat. Her long blond hair hung loose and lank around her shoulders. At least Britten thought it was blond; like the old man, she was extremely dirty, and it was hard to tell.

Men were following alongside the wagon, hooting and laughing. As the procession passed Jennings's tent, Deborah drew back slightly, as if offended by the sight.

"Who the devil is that?" Britten asked.

"The old man is named Mordecai Vint," Jennings explained. "He's a trader and peddler, I suppose you could say, although I'm not sure how he sells enough of that junk to support himself and the girl. I believe I heard someone say she's his granddaughter."

"Pathetic," Deborah said, but she did not sound overly sympathetic, at least not to Britten's ears.

"They've been following the railroad almost since we left Kansas City," Jennings said. "Every so often they disappear for a few days, and I think we're not going to be bothered with them anymore, but then they catch up to us again." The construction boss shook his head and lowered his voice. "I've also heard it said that he trades with the Indians. I suspect that's where they go when they drop out of sight. Vint's an old mountain man, like Sam Callaghan. He probably thinks we're ruining the country, too."

Britten nodded, his brow knitting in thought. If the rumors that Jennings had heard were true, Mordecai Vint might be the man for whom he was looking. Vint was not actually connected with the Kansas Pacific, but if he spent time around the camp, he could easily pick up valuable bits of knowledge to pass along to the Indians. And if he was indeed trading with them, he probably knew their language and felt fairly safe with them.

If Sam Callaghan was a suspect—and to Britten's way of thinking, he definitely was—then Mordecai Vint had to be put into that category as well. Britten decided to talk to Vint as soon as he had the appropriate opportunity. The man might let something slip if he thought he was talking to a potential customer.

Britten tipped his hat to Deborah and moved on toward the big tent that served as the dining hall. After he had eaten, he intended to spend the evening circulating through some of the saloons. Tonight would be the first chance he had to do that.

As Britten had expected, Osgood Newton was more than happy to have his young assistant join in the meal and conversation with the surveyors. Newton introduced Britten to the men, and within minutes Britten was absorbed in the discussion. The give-and-take was spirited as the men debated which route would be best for the railroad to follow. Of course, the general direction was already laid out, but the rights-of-way granted to the railroad covered enough territory to allow for quite a bit of leeway in the actual location of the roadbed. Britten was content to listen and keep his mouth shut; he had opinions of his own about the matter but little practical experience to lend weight to anything he might say.

Besides, he reminded himself, he was really there as an investigator, not an engineer.

Following the meal, Newton gestured at their surroundings, filled with noisy laborers, and said, "This is hardly the best place for such a discussion, gentlemen. What say we adjourn to my quarters?"

The other men nodded, and one of them said, "I'll bring the bottle, Ozzie."

Newton turned toward his newest worker and asked, "What about you, Britten? Will you join us again?"

Britten stood up from the bench beside the rough plank table. "I'm sorry, gentlemen," he said sincerely, "but I have other plans tonight."

"Another time, then," Newton said, and Britten nodded.

He would have liked to continue listening to what the men had to say, Britten thought as he strolled out through the flaps of the big tent, but he knew that he needed to stick to his plan of visiting some of the saloons. He was more likely to turn up some useful information there.

As he left the dining hall and turned toward the drinking establishments, he saw Mordecai Vint's wagon parked in front of the nearest one. There was no sign of the old man, but the light from the torches stuck in the ground near the saloon's entrance showed the dirty-faced young woman leaning against the wagon's front wheel.

Britten paused, watching her. One of the Irish tracklayers, weaving slightly from the whiskey he had obviously been putting away, approached her. The man spoke to her, and the young woman shook her head without looking up. The laborer said something else, and again she shook her head, more emphatically this time. Britten frowned slightly. He had a feeling the tracklayer was making some sort of indecent proposition to the woman, and when the man reached out and laid a heavy hand on her arm, Britten was sure of it. He started toward the wagon, acting on instinct.

But if Britten had planned on coming to the defense of the Vint woman, he had not needed to bother, he saw in the next few seconds. As soon as the drunken man grabbed the young woman's arm, her other hand darted under her long skirt and then flashed back out holding something. Britten saw the torchlight wink on the broad blade of a Bowie knife.

He stopped in his tracks, sure that in the next instant the girl would use the weapon to gut the man. But instead the tip of the blade stopped an inch away from the man's belly. The young woman said something in a low voice. Britten could not make out the words, but the man jerked away from her, sweat suddenly visible on his forehead. He wheeled around and moved quickly down the street.

When the woman saw Britten, who by now was standing only a few feet away, her angry eyes fastened on him. "What about you, mister?" she demanded in a hoarse voice, brandishing the knife. "You want to try a little of this?"

Britten held up both hands, palms out, and put a grin on his face. "Hell, no," he said. "I'm not looking for trouble."

"Well, you've found it if'n you aim to try sweet-talkin' me like that bastard."

"Wouldn't think of it," Britten assured her. "I just wanted to make sure he didn't bother you."

"Comin' to protect me, eh? I don't need no protection, mister. Got all I need right here." She lifted the knife again.

"I can see that."

He could see other things, too. She was young, as he had suspected, no more than twenty, and her hair was indeed blond under the coating of grease and grime. Her face was just as dirty as her hair, but the features were regular, and her blue eyes were sharp and alert.

"My name's Daniel Britten," he said quietly. He did not bother extending his hand. "What's yours?"

She glared suspiciously at him, still holding the knife. "Why do you want to know?"

Britten shrugged. "Curious, I guess."

She hesitated again, then said, "I'm Laura."

"Laura Vint?"

"That's my grandpappy's name. Reckon it's mine, too, but nobody ever calls me nothin' but Laura." Her mouth quirked in a bitter smile. "Less'n it's some dirty name. They call me those a lot when I tell 'em I ain't no whore."

"I knew that right away," Britten said. "Now, why don't you put that knife away?"

"You goin' to try anythin' funny?"

"Not a thing," Britten promised.

"All right, then." Laura Vint turned half away from Britten and replaced the Bowie somewhere under the folds of her tattered dress.

Britten pushed his hat onto the back of his head. "I hear that your grandfather is a trader," he said, wanting to keep the conversation going.

"He sure is. You want to buy somethin'?"

"Not right now, thanks. I imagine you've traveled quite a bit with him."

"Ever since my own folks up an' died of a fever when I was just a young 'un. Grandpappy took me in, right enough. Good folks do that for their kin."

Britten nodded. "Of course they do."

"Sure you don't want to buy somethin'?"

Britten pushed his hand into his pocket and found a few coins. "Come to think of it," he said, "I could use a new shaving mirror. I accidentally broke mine this morning."

Laura hurried around to the other side of the wagon, calling, "Just you wait a minute, mister." When she reappeared, she was carrying a round mirror, which she held out to Britten.

He took it and turned it over. The mirror had a small crack and was coated with dust, but it was usable. "That will do me just fine," he said. "How much do you want for it?"

"Grandpappy'd want two bits for it, was it him you was dealin' with." Laura looked down at the ground, but not before Britten saw a hint of a shy smile. "But seein' as he's inside drinkin' and left me to watch the wagon . . . hell, twenty cents'd be all right, I reckon."

Britten passed over the coins to her and said solemnly, "Thank you, Laura. Now, about that traveling you've done with your grandfather . . ."

"Yep, we been all over," she said proudly. "Kansas to the Dakotas an' ever'where in between. Grandpappy knows all the trails."

"I imagine he's met quite a few interesting people in his journeys, possibly even some Indians."

"Oh, hell, yes, we know them Injuns real good. Some of 'em are Grandpappy's pards from the old days, back when the fur trade was still good. I heard all the stories—"

She uttered a short, pained cry as Mordecai Vint stepped out of the shadows behind the wagon and jabbed a hard finger into her back. "Shut up, gal!" he barked. "Ain't I tol' you not to go spreadin' stories 'bout folks?"

Laura cringed away from him. "I'm sorry, Grandpappy," she said with a sob.

Vint's angry expression softened slightly when he saw the wetness in her eyes. "Aw, hell, Laura, I'm sorry, but you know you ain't supposed to go tellin' a man's business to strangers." The trader turned toward Britten and said with a scowl, "Speakin' of which, who the hell are you, mister, and why you pokin' your nose where it don't belong?"

"I didn't mean any harm," Britten said quickly. "I was just talking to your granddaughter. She seems like a nice girl—"

"She is a nice girl, dammit!" Vint blustered. "She ain't no whore, and I don't want you sons of bitches sniffin' 'round her. You understand me, boy?"

"I understand," Britten said coldly.

Laura clutched at the sleeve of her grandfather's ratty buffalo coat. "He weren't botherin' me, Grandpappy," she said. "Fact is, he was just about to run off some feller who was when I done the chore myself. Then he bought a mirror off'n the wagon. He's all right."

Vint's glare did not lessen. "Maybe so, but I still want you to keep your carcass away from this gal, mister."

"I told you I understand." With that, Britten turned away and stalked toward the tent saloon.

Inside he was seething. A fine detective he was! He might have been making a little progress with Laura Vint, but whatever opportunity had been there was now ruined, at least for the time being. If he had noticed Vint coming, he might have been able to turn the situation to his advantage. Instead, the trader had overheard Britten snooping into his activities. He was glad Matthew Faraday had not been there to witness that display of ineptitude.

Britten squared his shoulders and pushed into the saloon. The inside was dim and smoky, the scattered lanterns not doing much to relieve the gloom. The simple bar consisted of long planks laid atop kegs of whiskey, and men were lined up two and three deep, waiting for shots of the potent liquor. There were quite a few tables set up where gamblers plied their trade, and women with painted faces and gaudy dresses made their way through the crowd, picking out customers to take to the row of smaller tents out back. Shouts and laughter filled the air, but there was an air of desperation about the celebrating.

Britten waited patiently at the bar until he could get a mug of beer. The brew was hot and flat and bitter, but he sipped it anyway as he began to wander around the tent.

He stopped at one of the tables where a poker game was in progress and watched the play for a few minutes. As one hand drew to an end, two of the men threw in their cards disgustedly and stood up. "I'm through throwin' away my money!" one of them declared. "Think I'll go find me a gal."

His companion laughed. "Hell, that's throwin' it away, too," he said. "But I reckon I'll go with you anyway."

The gambler running the game glanced up. "Openings for a couple of players," he announced, raising his voice enough so that at least a few of the customers could hear him over the hubbub. His eyes lit on Britten. "How about you, mister?"

Just as Britten was about to shake his head, a familiar figure in buckskins pushed through the crowd and laid a hamlike hand on the back of one of the vacant chairs. "You don't want this little feller playin'," Sam Callaghan guffawed. "It might make his mama mad if she knew he was gamblin' with men." Stiffening, Britten glared up at Callaghan, but the brawny former mountain man was not deterred. Pulling out the chair, he said, "I'm in."

"And so am I," Britten added, pulling out the other chair and sitting down.

Callaghan shrugged his massive shoulders. "Up to you. Ain't nobody goin' to take pity on you 'cause you're wet behind the ears, though."

"That's fine with me."

The gambler leaned forward and said, "Welcome, gentlemen, both of you. Let's keep things civilized, shall we? The name's Jabez Mosely. I own this place."

The other men quickly introduced themselves. All of them were laborers, and that meant none of them could afford to be gambling away their wages in a tent saloon. But that was exactly what most of them did, Britten knew.

One of the workmen had the deal at the moment. He announced the game—seven-card stud—and began clumsily to pass out the cards. Britten watched carefully, but the man's awkwardness seemed to be natural, rather than any kind of cover for a crooked deal.

The hands went quickly once the game was under way. It took four hands before Britten won a pot, but that was not unusual; he had never been an exceptional poker player, even though he enjoyed the game itself.

Callaghan, on the other hand, seemed to have brought plenty of luck to the table with him. He lost the first hand, then proceeded to rake in a couple before Britten won. After that, Callaghan continued to win fairly often. When he did not, Jabez Mosely usually did.

After half an hour at the table Britten noticed that Mosely always won the largest pots. There were two possible explanations for that—either Mosely saved his best play for the most important hands, or he was cheating.

One of the tracklayers who had lost heavily seemed to think he had noticed something, too. Slamming down his cards, the man said, "Goddammit! What's a man have to do to get an honest hand around here?"

Callaghan, who had taken the last pot and now held the deck of cards, squinted at the man who had spoken and rumbled, "What the hell do you mean by that, mister?"

"I mean you're bottom dealing, you son of a bitch!"

Britten had been around enough railroad camps to know what was going to happen next. Unless he played a hunch of his own and surprised everyone . . .

Callaghan dropped the cards and started to roar as he jerked his hand toward the Dragoon holstered at his hip. But before Callaghan could complete the move, Britten lunged across the table, his fingers catching Mosely's arm and hanging on tightly. When the startled gambler tried to jerk back, his chair overturned with a crash.

"Look!" Britten rapped, using his other hand to snatch a hold-out card from Mosely's coat sleeve. "Here's your cheat!"

Mosely's expression had gone from a satisfied smirk to a mixture of rage and fear in a matter of seconds. He had probably been happy to see Callaghan accused of cheating; the resulting fracas would keep attention away from him. But now both Callaghan and the man who had accused him were turning toward him with furious faces.

"You duded-up little pissant!" Callaghan roared at Mosely. "I almost had to shoot this poor fool, when it was you doin' the cheatin'!"

For a second Mosely stared at Britten with hatred in his eyes, but then his other hand dove under his jacket and came out with a small pistol. "Wilbur!" he screamed.

Sam Callaghan upended the table just as the gambler's pocket pistol cracked, and the bullet thudded into the rough wood. The edge of the table hit Britten's wrist, forcing him to release Mosely. Callaghan shoved Britten from behind, sending him sprawling to the floor just as the second barrel of Mosely's gun blasted. The slug went wild, punching a hole in the side of the tent.

If not for the push from Callaghan, Britten realized as he lay on the hard-packed ground, the bullet would have hit him.

At the bar, the burly bartender who had been summoned by Mosely's cry leaped over the planks and started to push his way through the crowd. Several other men joined him. *Mosely's henchmen,* Britten thought as he saw them coming. He pushed himself up from the floor to meet their charge, but Sam Callaghan got there first.

The big man's fist lashed out and cracked against the bartender's jaw, knocking him back into his companions, several of whom went sprawling to the ground. Another man grabbed a bottle and started to bring it down on Callaghan's head.

The blow never arrived. Britten leaped forward, his right hand catching the man's wrist and stopping it in midair. Then he landed a jab to the man's solar plexus with his left, making the man gasp for air and turn pale. Britten jerked him closer and brought his knee up into the man's groin, doubling him over with pain.

Somebody landed on Britten's back, an arm looping around his throat and cutting off his air. Through the sudden roaring in his head, Britten heard angry shouts and yelps of pain and the crash of tables and chairs. A woman screamed.

Britten twisted his body and, letting himself fall onto the man who had jumped him, brought both of them to the floor, with himself on top. Driving his elbow back into the man's middle, Britten felt the man's grip loosen from around his neck, and he pulled himself free. He rolled to the side, narrowly missing being stomped by several pairs of boots.

As he surged up from the floor, he saw that the whole saloon had erupted into a brawling mob. There was nothing like a good fracas for blowing off steam. But Mosely and his men were taking it with deadly seriousness, Britten realized, when, behind the knot of struggling men around Sam Callaghan, he saw a knife flash.

The knife was in Jabez Mosely's hand, and the crooked gambler was advancing toward Callaghan, who had his hands full at the moment with three of Mosely's bouncers and could not see the danger. Britten stooped to pick up the leg of a chair that had been overturned and broken, and as he flung the makeshift club, he yelled, "Look out, Callaghan!"

A fist caught Britten from the side just as he shouted, knocking him down. He could not see the results of his attempt to save Callaghan's life, but he did hear a furious roar that sounded like thunder booming in the mountains.

When Britten sat up, he saw Mosely fly past, blood spurting from a pulped nose. The agent was trying to get up when hands grabbed his arms and he found himself being propelled rapidly toward the entrance of the tent.

Two of Mosely's men had a hold on him. He had time to see that much before he was suddenly sailing through the air into the street. Britten landed heavily, rolling over several times and trying to gulp air back into his lungs as he came up on hands and knees.

A second later four more men appeared in the tent's

entrance, lugging a massive form. They threw Sam Callaghan's unconscious figure toward Britten. The former mountain man had lost his hat during the fight, and his graying hair was in disarray and streaked with blood from a gash on his forehead.

One of the bouncers heaved a ragged breath and said, "Damn, I thought we were goin' to have to hit that old moose with an anvil 'fore he'd go down!"

Mosely stalked out of the tent, holding his pistol again. His other hand was pressed to his bleeding nose. He lifted the gun and leveled it at Britten.

"I should shoot both of you," Mosely said coldly. "I will if I ever see either one of you in my place again."

Britten took a deep breath and tried to keep a tight rein on his anger. "I don't like threats," he said flatly as he got to his feet.

"Then listen to a word of advice. If you come back, bring a gun with you."

"I'll do that."

"Now get your friend away from my place. I don't need trash like you in my doorway." With that, Mosely turned away and went back into the tent, but several of his men stood there to make sure that Britten did as he was told.

Britten knelt beside Callaghan and took hold of his thick arm. "Come on, Callaghan," Britten said. "Let's get out of here."

The big man, shaking his head and letting out a groan, pushed himself up on his hands and knees and onto his feet with a little assistance from Britten. He glared at the tent and started to take a step in that direction, muttering, "Nobody does that to Sam Callaghan."

"Just hold on," Britten insisted. "If you go back in there, Callaghan, they'll kill you. They damned near did us in the first time. There'll be a chance to even the score with Mosely later."

Callaghan hesitated, lifting his massive shoulders and clenching his fists as he sighed. "Reckon you're right." He winced suddenly and lifted a hand to his head. "What'd they use to hit me, anyway?"

"One of them said something about an anvil," Britten responded dryly.

"Feels like it, dammit."

Britten picked up his hat from the ground nearby and, grunting in pain as his muscles protested, turned back to Callaghan. "I suppose I should thank you. You saved my life when Mosely cut loose at me with that pistol."

"You returned the favor," Callaghan replied. "That chair leg you flung smacked Mosely a good 'un. Just as he was about to stick me, too. 'Preciate it."

"He seemed to think you and I were friends."

Callaghan gave Britten his usual squinty-eyed glare. "Don't know as I'd go so far as to say that. But you got sand in your craw, youngster. I'll give you that."

Britten grinned. "Come on," he said, coming to a decision. "We'll stop at another of these saloons and pick up a bottle. It's a little more peaceful back at my tent."

Callaghan pondered the offer for a moment, then nodded. "Sounds all right to me."

Britten made a mental note of the cost of the bottle of whiskey, since sharing it with Callaghan would make it qualify as a legitimate expense to report to Matthew Faraday. He felt grateful for the way Callaghan had pitched in during the fight, but the evening's events certainly did not eliminate the big man as a suspect.

When they were back in Britten's tent and had passed the bottle back and forth a couple of times, Britten said, "Why did you turn the table over when Mosely pulled his gun? You didn't have to save my life."

"Hell, you didn't have to show up Mosely for a cheat, neither. You could've let me and that yack go to shootin' at each other. How'd you know Mosely was cheatin', anyway?"

"I noticed the way he was winning all of the biggest pots," Britten said. "And every time he did, he was only drawing one card. Seemed likely to me he was hiding cards, but I was really just playing a hunch."

Callaghan laughed. "Well, it was a good one. Reckon we both made some enemies tonight, but I ain't goin' to lose much sleep over snakes like Mosely."

"Me neither," Britten declared. He took another swig from the bottle and then handed it back to Callaghan. It was time to change the subject, he decided. "Somebody told me you'd spent some time living with the Indians. That must have been fascinating."

Callaghan drank and then nodded. "Them was shinin' times, I'll tell you that. The Injuns really knowed how to live off the land without upsettin' it. They take what they need and leave the rest alone. An Injun ain't greedy, Britten. Not like a white man, who just wants more and more and don't give a damn how he gets it."

"I can sure sympathize with the Indians," Britten said. "If I were one of them, I wouldn't want the railroad coming through, either. I don't suppose there's any way to stop it in the long run, though. You can't hold back progress."

"Progress, hell!" Callaghan snorted. "Progress ain't nothin' except takin' a thing that works and fixin' it where it don't." He gestured at the buckskin jacket he wore. "You take this here. The Injuns taught me how to make buckskins, and I been wearin' 'em ever since. Always skin out the bucks and make my own. Last for years and years, and they're right comfortable. But I hear tell you can go in stores back east now and buy the things ready-made. Ain't that a hell of a note! Bet they fall apart in six months."

Britten laughed. "I take it you don't care for storebought goods."

"Never had 'em where I come from, never had no need of 'em. Hell, youngster, I never even been to Kansas City, and that's just fine with me."

"You've lived all your life on the frontier?"

Callaghan nodded. "Damned right. And I'll die out here, too." He held out the bottle to Britten. "Have another snort of this who-hit-John."

As Britten drank deeply, he thought about everything he had learned that night. On the surface, it did not amount to a great deal. He knew now that Mordecai Vint was pretty secretive about his actions away from the railhead, and he had confirmed the fact that Sam Callaghan was opposed in principle to the road's expansion.

And he had found himself liking Callaghan. The man was abrasive and opinionated and did not give a damn whose feathers he ruffled, but he was also a good man to have at his back in a fight, Britten now knew.

That did not matter, he told himself. If Sam Callaghan was guilty, Britten vowed that he would bring the big man to justice.

Chapter 7

OVER THE NEXT FEW DAYS DANIEL BRITTEN LEARNED THAT
Callaghan and Vint were not the only men in camp
with a grudge against the railroad. He continued his
practice of listening in on the conversations in the
dining hall and the saloons, and it soon became
obvious that many of the workers were unhappy with
their situation. In addition to not making much
money, they were being pushed almost to their limits.
If the camp did have a traitor who was motivated solely by revenge, then Britten had to admit that
there were dozens of possible suspects from whom
to choose. None of the workers had the free-
dom of movement that Callaghan and Vint did, however.

Britten was aware that revenge might not be the
only motive in the case; money could be equally
important. If Indian resistance forced the Kansas
Pacific to alter its route significantly, new right-of-way
deals would be required. That could mean a fortune
for anyone lucky enough to own land along the new
route.

Lucky enough—or ruthless enough to see to it that

the route had to be changed.

So far there had been no Indian attacks during Britten's stay at the railhead, and he was a little surprised by that. But he felt certain that the peace would not last.

He was in Osgood Newton's tent working on one of the maps when the chief draftsman came in with a man Britten recognized as one of the surveyors. The man wore a suit, stiff collar, and tie, and he had a neatly trimmed beard.

"Britten, I think you know Mr. Arbuthnot," Newton said.

Britten nodded and stood up. "Hello, sir. Good to see you again."

"Do you feel up to a little trip, Britten?" Arbuthnot asked, his voice carrying the brisk tones of New England.

Britten's pulse quickened. "I suppose so, sir. Why do you ask?"

Newton came around the table and sat down. "Mr. Arbuthnot and his surveying crew are going out today, Britten. I want you to go with them."

Before Britten could say anything, Arbuthnot asked, "Can you ride?"

"Yes, sir," Britten replied. "I've been on surveying trips before."

"Excellent. We'll be pulling out just after noon. You'll need drafting paper and your pens, of course." Arbuthnot paused for a moment, then added, "And a gun, if you've got one."

"I've got one," Britten said. "Are you expecting trouble from the Indians?"

"With the way things have been around here lately, only a fool wouldn't be."

Newton spoke up. "I know we haven't had any trouble while you've been here, Britten, but that's less than a week. The savages sometimes like to try to lull us to sleep, so that they can do more damage when they do strike."

"And I'd say it's getting close to time again,"

Arbuthnot commented. He nodded to Britten and went on. "I'll see you later." Then he turned and left the tent.

Britten straightened up the work he had left on the table, then said, "I guess I'd better go get my things ready. How long do you think we'll be gone, Mr. Newton?"

"Two days, at least, possibly longer," Newton replied. His voice softened a bit as he went on. "Be careful out there, Daniel. Arbuthnot's a good man, and so are the others, but we are due for some trouble."

"I'll keep my eyes open," Britten promised.

And my Starr revolver handy, he added silently to himself.

Arbuthnot was in charge of the surveying party, which was comprised of four men besides Britten. The second-in-command was another surveyor, named Maxwell, and there were two assistants, Forbes and Lancomb. Britten was slightly acquainted with all of them.

He ate an early lunch and then drew a horse from the small remuda that traveled with the railhead. When he arrived at Arbuthnot's tent, he found the party ready to pull out.

"Do you have everything you need?" Arbuthnot asked.

Britten held up a small case that contained a thick sheaf of drawing paper and his set of pens. "I have my drafting equipment," he said, "and this." He pushed back his coat to reveal the pistol holstered on his hip.

"Very good." Arbuthnot raised his voice. "Mount up, men."

As the five men swung into their saddles, Britten said, "Is one of the scouts going with us? Sam Callaghan, maybe?"

Arbuthnot snorted contemptuously. "That uneducated ruffian? We don't need him along causing trouble. I know my way around this country."

Britten glanced at the other men and sensed that

they did not completely share Arbuthnot's confidence. The surveyor might know the country, but Callaghan was a tough, experienced fighter.

But as Arbuthnot prodded his horse into motion, the others fell in behind him and rode west, following the newly laid tracks.

When they had covered several miles, the actual railhead came into sight. Gangs of men were laboring under the hot Kansas sun, building up the roadbed, hauling ties, laying rails, and driving spikes. Britten spotted Terence Jennings standing on a handcar several yards behind the spot where the tracks ended.

As the surveying party rode up, Jennings took his hat off and mopped sweat from his brow. "Hello!" he called. "I see you're setting out again, Mr. Arbuthnot."

"That's what the Kansas Pacific pays me for," the stern New Englander said. "We'll be back in a couple of days with some better maps of the Big Creek area."

"Good." Jennings nodded. "Then the engineers can finish the final details of those trestle plans. Keep an eye out for Indians." The construction boss glanced over at Britten and grinned. "I see you're going to get a look at some new country, Daniel."

"That's right," Britten acknowledged. "I'm looking forward to it."

"You still haven't had dinner with Deborah and me," Jennings reminded him. "When you get back, you'll have to join us and tell us about the territory up ahead. I'm sure Deborah would enjoy that."

Britten nodded. "I'll do that," he said, although he was unsure he would keep the promise.

Waving to Jennings and the other men, the surveying crew headed west. As he rode, Britten thought about Deborah Rowland. He had not been consciously avoiding her, but he had not seen her in the last few days. He still felt some embarrassment that he had been in her bed with her only hours before she was reunited with the man she intended to marry, but whatever guilt he had experienced had faded away; the romantic night in Deborah's private car had been as much her idea as his, maybe more so. Nevertheless, he felt slightly uncomfortable around her. If she had not been so damned beautiful, he might have been able to put her out of his mind entirely.

Just as Arbuthnot had said, he had been over this ground before, when the general route for the railroad had been laid out. Occasionally the chief surveyor would call a halt, and the crew would set up its instruments to take measurements. Britten's job, he rapidly discovered, was to sketch rough maps onto which he recorded those measurements. Later, when the group returned to the camp, the details from these small maps would be transferred to the much larger ones drawn by Osgood Newton.

They were traveling through the broad gentle valley of the Smoky Hill River, which lay to the south of them. The Smoky Hills were to their north. Arbuthnot pointed out a stubby sort of hill jutting up from the plains far to the west, and he explained to Britten, "That's Round Mound. Not much of a peak, but it's what passes for a mountain out here. Before the railroad reaches it, the route must twice cross Big Creek, which also belies its name to a certain extent. Neither of the two trestles will be any great feat of engineering, mind you, but it's still important that you get all of our measurements down correctly."

"I will, sir," Britten nodded. "Don't worry."

As they rode, Britten found himself keeping an eye on the low hills to the north, where he felt sure Sioux and Cheyenne were hiding, watching the surveyors' progress. The question was, would they come out and pay a visit to such a small group of white men riding across the prairie?

In the late afternoon, when the group reached a good-sized bowl in the land, Arbuthnot called a halt. "We'll camp here," he said. "The savages won't spot our fires in this depression."

Britten was not so sure of that, but he did not want to argue with Arbuthnot. After the men had dismounted, Maxwell built a small fire while Forbes and

Lancomb tended to the horses. Arbuthnot immediately sat down cross-legged on the ground and pulled a notebook from his coat pocket. He began scribbling notes in it with a pencil stub, using what was left of the rapidly fading light.

If he had been in charge, Britten thought, he would have made a cold camp. As the shadows dropped down on the prairie, he felt icy fingers move along his spine. He had the unmistakable sensation of being watched.

Sliding the Starr from its holster, he checked the loads in the cylinder and hefted the weight of the weapon in his hand. It made him feel a little better, but not much. Despite his nervousness about the fire, the cup of hot coffee he sipped during the meal was most welcome.

When the group was through eating, Arbuthnot said, "I suppose we should post a guard and take turns standing watch. Any volunteers for the first shift?"

"I'll do it," Maxwell said, grinning in the glow from the fire. "I'd rather stay up a little later than crawl out of my bedroll in the middle of the night."

The men arranged the other watches, and Britten drew the two-to-four-o'clock shift, since that was the least desirable one and he was the newcomer.

He might as well have volunteered to stand guard the entire night, he thought as he lay in his bedroll later, trying to sleep. He was restless, hearing every little sound in the night and reading ominous messages into them, but nothing happened during his watch nor the other times, and morning dawned peacefully.

Britten rubbed his tired eyes, gulped down more coffee, biscuits, and bacon, then mounted up with the others. As they continued westward, the gently rolling hills gradually sloped upward. Britten could still see Round Mound in the distance, seemingly no closer than it had been the day before.

The party reached Big Creek in midmorning and stopped to let Arbuthnot and Maxwell take a long series of readings and measurements. Britten, who had little to do while the two surveyors and their assistants were setting up their equipment, noticed a slight rise to the north. He went over to Arbuthnot and said, "I think I'll ride up on that ridge and have a look around, if that's all right with you, sir."

Arbuthnot nodded absently. "That's probably a good idea," he said. "Make sure there are no savages in the vicinity. But your services will be required back here in approximately half an hour."

"I'll be back by then," Britten promised, and he started to turn his horse away.

"Hold on a moment," Arbuthnot called, and reaching over to his saddlebag, he pulled out a small spyglass, which he handed to Britten. "In case you spot any hostiles, you can get a better look at them with this."

"Thanks," Britten said. He slipped the instrument into his own saddlebag.

Spurring the horse into a trot, he quickly reached the top of the rise. It was not much of an elevation, but on this mostly flat land, any rise enabled a man to see a good distance. Slowly turning his horse, Britten scanned the horizon in every direction from where he sat in his saddle.

Far to the north, a flicker of motion caught his eye. Britten took out the spyglass, lifted it, and, squinting through the instrument, saw the scene spring into sharp focus. A lone rider was heading west, and a hundred yards in front of him several other men on horseback were riding toward him. The members of this group wore buckskins, feathers, and war paint.

The lone rider was white, and Britten caught his breath as he recognized him: Sam Callaghan.

Callaghan, his right hand lifted in a gesture of peace, rode right up to the approaching Indians. Britten frowned, his grip tightening on the spyglass as he saw Callaghan, sitting easily in his saddle, talk to the Indians in a calm manner. From the markings on their faces, Britten determined that the Indians were Sioux.

Britten's mind was racing. What the hell was Callaghan doing out there, miles from the railhead, having a secret meeting with a band of Indians? The same answer kept coming back to Britten—he had very likely found his traitor.

Since he could do nothing about it now, he put the spyglass in his saddlebag and wheeled his horse, heading back toward Big Creek and the surveying party. As he rode, he tried to compose himself so that the jumble of emotions he was feeling would not show on his face.

He had come to like Sam Callaghan—well, not *like,* perhaps, but at least he had respected the burly old scout. At least he had until today.

"Any sign of trouble?" Arbuthnot asked as Britten rode up.

"No," Britten answered, his face and voice revealing nothing. "No trouble at all."

During the afternoon Britten did his work carefully and correctly. The group moved on later, riding several more miles to where Big Creek's curve brought it back across the route of the railroad. Again Arbuthnot and his men took their measurements, and Britten noted them precisely. They camped that night near Round Mound, which had finally become more than a distant landmark.

As he was eating a rude dinner that evening, Britten considered telling Arbuthnot that he had spotted some Indians that morning. He wished he had told him at the time and just left out any mention of Sam Callaghan, but his mind had been in such a turmoil that it had not occurred to him. Now it was too late to say anything without making Arbuthnot and the others suspicious of him. *And with good reason,* he thought.

The men were just finishing their meal when the sound of hooves made them drop their plates and cups and reach for their weapons. Britten slipped the Starr from its holster and turned slightly to face the night. The creak of wagon wheels came to his ears.

"Halloooo, the camp!" came a raspy, familiar voice hailing them from the shadows. "All right to come in?"

"Vint," Arbuthnot said disgustedly, letting the rifle in his hands sag toward the ground. He called, "Come ahead!"

Britten heard the jangling of the items on the wagon, and a moment later Mordecai Vint, as filthy as ever, drove his disreputable old vehicle into the circle of light cast by the fire. Laura was beside him on the seat.

Vint hauled his mules to a stop and got down, leaving Laura to manage for herself.

When Britten stepped forward to offer her his arm, she glared at him and asked, "What's that for?"

"I just thought I'd help you down," he said.

Laura jumped lithely from the wagon seat. "I can get down by myself."

Vint strode up to the fire and wiped a paw across his mouth. "Any chance o' gettin' some grub from you good folks?" he asked Arbuthnot.

The surveyor's features were stiff with distaste as he replied, "You're welcome to share our fire and what provisions we have, Vint. Just stay downwind as much as possible, please."

The old trader grinned. "Hell, you can't hurt my feelin's like that, mister. Figgered you'd know that by now." He sat down cross-legged by the fire, his huge buffalo coat spread on the ground around him, and reached out to snare a biscuit from the pan. His other hand emerged from beneath the coat holding the neck of a whiskey bottle. He gnawed a bite of the biscuit, washed it down with a long, gurgling swallow of the fiery liquor, then said, "Seen any Injun sign?"

"Not so far," Arbuthnot answered.

"They're out there," Vint said confidently. "You

may not see 'em, but they're there. Maybe they'll leave you alone tonight, though, if'n you're lucky."

On the other side of the fire, Britten said to Laura, "Can I get you something to eat?"

She followed her grandfather's example, sitting down on the ground and helping herself. "Look, mister," she said in a low voice, "you was nice to me back at the camp, and I 'preciate that. But it don't change nothin'. I'm still who I am, and you're still who you are, and we ain't got one damned reason to be friendly to each other."

Britten shrugged. "Suit yourself. I was just trying to help."

"Well, don't."

He hesitated a moment, then said to her, "What are the two of you doing way out here, anyway? You're a long way from the railhead."

For a long moment Britten thought she was not going to answer. Then, in a low voice that Vint would not be able to hear, she said, "Grandpappy's been off doin' some tradin'. We don't make enough off them railroad folks to keep a hog in shit."

"Oh." Britten took a deep breath and went on. "Doing some trading with the Indians, was he?"

Laura snorted. "Hell of a lot you know. Injuns got no money. All they can trade you is some buffalo hides or maybe a few stole horses. But there's ranchers 'round here, too."

Britten frowned. He had heard that a few hardy souls were trying to establish ranches on the Kansas plains, but he did not know whether any of them had been successful. "I didn't know this was ranching country," he said.

"Oh, hell, yes," Laura said around a mouthful of biscuit. "There's a whole passel of spreads 'tween here and the Rockies. Grandpappy makes the rounds of 'em. The Injuns don't bother 'em much; them heathens are more worried 'bout stoppin' the railroad."

Several yards away, her grandfather glared at her

and snapped, "What you yammerin' about over there, gal? Ain't you learned yet that a female's got no business openin' her mouth?"

Laura muttered an apology, then sent a scowl in Britten's direction, as if she were blaming him for the scolding she had received. He stood up and moved away, well aware that Vint's hostile eyes were following him.

So Vint had been out there away from the railhead, too. Just when Britten had made up his mind that Sam Callaghan was the villain, Mordecai Vint popped up again. Granted, there was more evidence against Callaghan—that meeting with the Indians was pretty damned incriminating—but Vint could not be ignored, either.

The trader gulped some coffee, then said, "We're headin' back to the railhead tomorrow. Reckon we could travel along with you folks? More guns that way in case of a run-in with the Injuns."

"All right," Arbuthnot said, nodding.

Britten glanced up at the brilliant stars overhead, trying to mask his pleasure about Vint's decision to accompany them. Keeping an eye on the old man would be far easier that way.

And he had a feeling that Mordecai Vint warranted the attention.

Chapter 8

THE SURVEYING PARTY SAW NO SIGN OF ANYONE, INDIAN OR otherwise, as they returned to the construction camp the next day over the same ground they had covered on the journey out. Britten would not have minded talking again to Laura Vint to relieve the tedium, but she was sitting on the wagon next to her grandfather, and it was obvious old Mordecai did not like the young draftsman.

Besides, Britten thought Laura also seemed cool toward him now. He wondered if it was because she got in trouble with her grandfather every time she talked to him. Vint certainly acted like a man with something to hide.

Britten sensed that Laura might prove to be a source of valuable information, but that was not his only reason for wishing he could get closer to her. He was also wondering what she would look like if all of the dirt was scrubbed off and she was dressed in decent clothes.

By four o'clock that afternoon they were within an

hour's ride of the railhead. Britten glanced up sharply as Lancomb called out, "Rider coming."

Britten saw the lone rider approaching, still far enough away that he could not make out the man's identity. Arbuthnot snapped, "Britten, are you any good with that gun?"

"I get by," he replied.

"Then come with me. I want to see who that is. The rest of you stay here and be ready for trouble." The surveyor spurred ahead without looking back to see if Britten was following his orders.

Prodding his horse into a trot, Britten soon caught up with Arbuthnot, and the men rode side by side. Britten noticed the surveyor's face was calm and composed, even though they might be riding into danger.

They recognized the newcomer at the same time, and as Arbuthnot reined in, he said in tones that hinted at his relief, "Look, Britten, it's only Jennings." He turned in his saddle and waved the others to come on ahead.

A moment later Terence Jennings rode up to them, cuffing his hat back and grinning. "Afternoon," he greeted them. "Any trouble, Mr. Arbuthnot?"

"None at all," Arbuthnot answered. "And I believe you'll find that we have completed the measurements needed for the Big Creek trestles in good form, sir."

"I knew I could count on you." Jennings smiled at Britten. "Well, Daniel, are you disappointed you didn't get to fight the redskins?"

"Not one damned bit," Britten answered honestly with a chuckle. "I didn't sign on with the Kansas Pacific to trade shots with Indians."

"None of us did."

Jennings's presence out there away from the railhead puzzled Britten, and he asked, "Did you ride out to meet us, Mr. Jennings?"

The construction boss laughed humorlessly. "I knew you'd probably be coming in, but that's not the real reason I left the camp. To tell the truth, I wanted to get away from the uproar for a few minutes."

"Uproar?" Arbuthnot questioned.

"We've got visitors in camp," Jennings replied flatly. "A bunch of cowboys from some of the ranches around here decided they needed some hell-on-wheels liquor and women. They've been celebrating for nearly twenty-four hours now, and the railroad workers don't like it much."

Arbuthnot nodded. "I've seen such cowboy debaucheries before, I'm afraid. You may be in for trouble, Jennings."

Britten frowned as Vint's wagon and the rest of the surveying party came up. If the situation was as bad as Jennings and Arbuthnot made it sound, then why had Jennings gone off and left Deborah there alone? Of course, it was unlikely that any of the men, laborers and cowboys alike, would molest her even if they were drunk, but it still seemed like an unnecessary danger.

Britten was about to say something to that effect when Jennings turned his horse and said, "We'd better get back. No telling what hell is breaking loose."

Their pace picked up the closer they got to the camp. As they rode in, Britten saw extra horses tied around the tent saloons and heard whoops of drunken laughter coming from inside.

Arbuthnot said, "Come along, Britten. We'll deliver our information to Newton and let him get started on his work."

Britten nodded, although he really wanted to go check on Deborah. Then he saw Jennings riding toward Deborah's tent and realized it was better that her fiancé check on her, anyway.

Newton was happy with the sketches Britten turned over to him, and as he flipped through them, he grunted, "Good work. Why don't you relax for the rest of the day, Britten?"

"I'd be glad to," Britten said sincerely. He had a

great deal to think over, and he might be able to do it better over a cold beer.

The beer was not very cold in the tent saloon he selected, but it was wet and slid easily down his parched throat. The place was packed, and he had to wait in line for the drink, but it was worth it.

As he looked around, he saw that at least a dozen of the visiting cowboys were in the room. They were rowdy and happy, thoroughly enjoying themselves and ignoring the glares coming their way from the railroad workers. But as dusk fell, more and more workers entered the saloon, and then the tension grew more apparent.

Britten had seen no sign of Sam Callaghan since returning to the camp, and when he asked the bartender about the big scout, the man said, "Ain't seen him for a day or two, don't reckon. But that ain't unusual for Sam. He spends a lot of time off by himself."

An outburst of laughter drew Britten's attention. Several cowhands were playing cards at a table with four of the railroad workers, and judging from the hilarity coming from the cowboys, one of them had just won a sizable pot. A lean man in a Stetson and chaps stood up with a grin on his face and a wad of money in his hand. "Be seein' you boys later," he said, and he strolled off to spend his winnings.

Britten moved forward quickly, sliding into the empty chair before anyone else could claim it. He looked around the table and said, "I think I'll play a hand or two, if it's all right with everyone."

"All right with me," one of the railroad workers said with a grunt, and the others nodded assent. "Leastways you ain't one of them cow nurses."

The game was five-card stud this time, and Britten saw right away that he was not going to be drawing good cards tonight. But that was not why he had taken the seat. The cowboys and the ranches they represented were a new factor in the case he was investigating, and sitting in on this poker game might give him a chance to learn more about the situation.

The cowboys talked and laughed among themselves as they played, but most of the railroad workers were sullen and silent. The cowboys seemed to be winning more, too, and that only increased the laborers' resentment. Britten watched the cards closely but saw no evidence of cheating; the luck of the cowboys was just better tonight.

As one of the punchers reached out to rake in a sizable pot, a railroad worker grabbed his wrist to stop him and growled, "Hold it, mister. I ain't satisfied that hand was on the up and up."

Immediately the cowboys' good mood vanished. "No call to talk like that, friend," the challenged cowboy said coolly. "It's just the luck of the draw, nothing more."

"I ain't so sure."

Stiffly, the cowboy said, "Either say what you've got to say or get your damned paw off me, mister."

Britten leaned forward. "We don't want trouble around here, boys," he interjected. "This is supposed to be a friendly game."

"I'm sayin' you and your friends are cheats," the laborer insisted, ignoring Britten's cautionary words.

The cowboy jerked his hand loose, leaving the money on the table and reaching instead for his gun. Britten bit back a curse and used the same strategy Sam Callaghan had employed in Mosely's saloon—he turned the table over.

The railroad worker lunged for the cowboy's throat, knocking aside the big Colt, while the other players leaped into the melee, fists and feet flying. Howls of outrage filled the air.

Britten was in the middle of it. Dodging punches thrown by cowboys and laborers alike, he dropped to the floor in an attempt to get away from the knot of struggling men.

As he came to his feet, he saw one of the railroad workers scoop up a bottle from the floor and swing it toward the head of a cowhand. Britten dived forward, grasping the trackman's hand and bearing down on his arm. Thrown off balance, the man staggered, and Britten hooked a boot behind his knee. The trackman went crashing to the ground, the bottle slipping from his hand and rolling away. As the downed man tried to regain his feet, Britten's fist cracked into his jaw.

When the stunned railroad man slumped back to the dirt, the cowboy glanced over his shoulder and had time to grin and say "Thanks!" to Britten before he had to duck a flying chair.

Something crashed into Britten from behind. He went down to one knee and twisted as a railroad worker clubbed at him with both fists. His quick action to save the cowboy from a broken skull had been noticed, and now the trackmen were against him. Even though he worked for the railroad, they did not consider him one of them and never would.

Britten blocked the punches and shot back one of his own, his knuckles banging into the jaw of his attacker. The man spun away with a glassy look in his eyes, but another worker took his place in an instant.

Within minutes the brawl boiled down to a group of cowboys in the center of the big tent surrounded by angry railroad workers, whom the cowboys were holding off as best they could. Britten stood with the cowboys, slugging it out toe to toe with the railroad men who came at him. A cut on his cheek was trickling blood into his mouth, and one eye was swelling a little from a blow, but overall he felt surprisingly good.

He smashed one of the men away from him and was setting himself to ward off another when the blast of a shotgun made everyone freeze. Britten saw Terence Jennings stride into the tent, a shotgun in his hands. The construction boss said, in a voice that seemed loud in the sudden silence, "I've got another barrel here if anyone wants it."

The battlers stood quiet and still, none of them sure how serious Jennings was with his threat.

"That's better," Jennings said after a moment. "You men who work for the Kansas Pacific—out of here, right now!"

There was quite a bit of grumbling, but the railroad workers slowly filed out of the tent. Britten stayed where he was, standing with the cowboys.

Jennings approached the group of embattled punchers, letting the barrels of the shotgun droop slightly. His eyes showed his surprise when he noticed Britten.

"What are you doing here, Daniel?" he asked.

"I was just having a drink and playing some poker, Mr. Jennings, when all of a sudden I was on the wrong side in a fight I didn't want."

One of the cowboys spoke up. "If this feller works for you, mister, don't be too hard on him. He tried to stop the fight before it got started good. But one o' them micks had his mind made up we was cheatin'."

"Were you?" Jennings asked flatly.

"No, sir, we wasn't."

Jennings sighed. His face was set in tired lines. "Well, I don't suppose it really matters. From now on, the construction camp is off limits to you men. I want you to pass along that news to the other ranches in the area, too."

"Off limits?" another cowboy yelped in protest. "You can't do that, mister!"

The bartender, who was also the owner of the saloon, chimed in, "That's right, Jennings. You got no right. I can sell liquor to anybody I please."

Jennings turned to face the bar. "You're operating on Kansas Pacific right-of-way, and I can do anything I damned well please. Maybe I don't have any authority over these cowboys, but if they don't stay away, I can sure order my workers not to come into these places."

"You'd have a mutiny on your hands right quick," the bartender scoffed.

Jennings patted the stock of the shotgun and said, "I don't think so."

Britten watched the construction boss with admiration. Jennings was facing up to a tough situation and not backing down an inch. Although the bartender protested and the cowboys did not like the idea, Britten figured that Jennings would get his way.

The cowboy who seemed to be the spokesman for the group finally said, "Reckon we don't want trouble, mister. How about lettin' us have one last drink before you run us off, though?"

Jennings nodded. "I don't suppose that would hurt anything."

The cowboy laid a hand on Britten's shoulder. "Come on, mister. You may work for this here iron-horse outfit, but I'd like to buy you a drink anyway."

Britten wiped blood off his face and grinned. "I'll take it."

After Jennings had left the saloon with a stern warning for the cowboys to remember what he had said—one drink, and then they would leave and not come back—Britten sat down at a table with a couple of the punchers. His mind was turning over rapidly. This fracas could be a blessing in disguise. He had wanted to get to know the cowboys, and the fight had accomplished that. They now regarded him as an ally.

One of the men got a bottle and glasses from the bar and brought them back to the table. As the drinks were poured, the cowboy who had invited Britten to join them stuck out his hand and said, "Name's Gebhardt—Charlie Gebhardt."

"Daniel Britten." The agent returned the handshake. "I'm glad to meet you."

"Not as glad as I am. Don't know if you noticed during all the commotion, but that was my head the feller was about to bash in when you stopped him." Gebhardt grinned. "Have to admit, I'm surprised you sided with us, Britten. Railroad folks usually stick together."

"I'm afraid the tracklayers don't regard me as one of them," Britten said. "I'm a draftsman. I work with the surveyors and engineers."

"Well, you pack a good punch for a pencil pusher, I'll give you that."

Britten sipped his whiskey and said, "I didn't know there were any ranches around here."

"Hell, yes," one of the other men said. "There's a bunch of spreads north of here. It's prime grazin' land. Why else do you think all them buffalo are around?"

"Most of us come up here from Texas when the rails reached Abilene," Gebhardt said. "We were part of the bunch that brought the longhorns up the trails. The boys and me didn't have no real reason to go back, so we hooked up with outfits tryin' to get a start here in Kansas."

"How are the ranches doing?" Britten asked, trying to appear only idly curious.

"Not bad, most of them. Lot of the spreads are growin'. Things are gettin' better since the owners started the association."

"What association?"

"The Great Plains Cattlemen's Association," Gebhardt said. "Most of the stockmen in the area got together with some fellers who own interests in the land, and they're workin' to make sure this here railroad does right by them."

Britten nodded. He wondered if the Great Plains Cattlemen's Association was working on anything else. An organization of ranchers and land speculators would have a prime motive for wanting to affect the route of the Kansas Pacific. If the railroad had to veer northward, it would run right through the heart of the ranching country, and the area would boom—not to mention the money the speculators would make from the land deals that would be required.

His pulse racing, Britten tried not to let the excitement show on his face. Every instinct he had told him he was on the right trail, that Amos Rowland's hunch had been right all along. Someone in the camp had to be working for the cattlemen's association in an effort to impede the road's progress. That someone, Britten thought, was probably either Sam Callaghan or Mordecai Vint—or maybe both of them, he suddenly realized. There would be nothing stopping the land syndicate from having two agents.

Britten took a deep breath and downed the rest of his drink. "I appreciate it, boys," he said, pushing his chair back. "But I just got back from a surveying trip today, and I'm pretty tuckered out. So I think I'll be moving along."

"Reckon we'd better pull out, too," Gebhardt said, "before that boss of yours comes back with his shotgun."

Britten said his farewells and went to the tent's entrance, pushing out through the flap. He really was tired, but he had a feeling that he would not sleep much that night; he had too much to think about.

He headed for his tent, his mind whirling. There had to be a way to put a stop to the trouble, and exposing the traitor might not be enough.

He was so engrossed in his thoughts that he did not hear the rush of feet until the men were nearly on him. Then he jerked his head around and saw the three figures lunging at him.

He tried to throw himself to the side, but a hand caught his arm and yanked him around roughly. A second man grabbed his other arm, pinning him between them as a fist slammed brutally into his middle.

"Hold him good and tight," the man who had hit Britten growled. "We'll teach the little bastard a lesson!"

Pain engulfed Britten. He tasted bile in the back of his throat, mixed with the whiskey. Again the man hit him, driving his fist deep into Britten's belly, but as a spasm of vomiting wracked Britten, the attacker stepped back quickly.

"Don't let him choke on it," the man snapped. "We don't want him dead, just hurtin'."

As Britten hung between the two men, he thought

desperately that despite what the man had just said, many more punches like that would be fatal. He had to get loose before they beat him to death.

They had come out of the shadows between two tents, and in that split second, Britten had recognized them as three of the men from the fight in the saloon. This was their way of paying him back for siding with the cowboys, he knew.

He let his weight sag completely, as if he had passed out. Then, somehow making his right leg work, he lashed out across his body, aiming his boot at the crotch of the man on his left. The kick connected; there was not much power behind it, but it was strong enough to make the man cry out in pain and release Britten's arm.

He twisted. Since none of them had expected him to fight back, his reaction had taken them by surprise, and now that his left arm was free, he was able to send a fist into the face of the other man holding him. The man fell backward.

But before Britten could turn around, the third man, the one who had already dealt him so much punishment, smashed him in the back of the neck with clubbed fists. Britten was driven down onto the ground, slumped on his face. Then a boot thudded into his side, making him grunt in agony and try to curl up into a smaller target.

They were going to stomp him to death now. It had gone too far to have any other outcome.

The blast of a shot ripped through the night. A part of Britten's brain recognized it as the sound of a Colt Dragoon. Sam Callaghan carried a Dragoon—

"Watch it! She's crazy!"

"Let's get outta here!"

Britten heard the frantic words come from the men who had been trying to kill him, followed by the pounding of running feet. He tried to push himself up on hands and knees but could not make it. There was dirt in his mouth, and he could not seem to spit it out.

Then someone was kneeling beside him, turning

him over, helping him to sit up. Blinking, Britten saw that it was Laura Vint, and that she held a heavy pistol in one hand. Smoke drifted up from the Colt's barrel.

"You all right?" she asked.

Britten clasped his left arm across his middle, trying to hold in the pain. "I . . . I will be," he said raggedly, "thanks . . . to you."

"You're a lucky son of a bitch," Laura said. "If I hadn't been passin' by, them fellers would've stomped your guts out."

"I know. I think they made a good start at it."

Laura stood up. "Can you walk?"

"I think so." With her help, Britten got back on his feet and took a staggering step.

She studied his face in the light from a nearby lantern. "You're all banged up," she said.

"That's from earlier. There was a fight in the saloon. This time they only hit me in the back of the neck and the stomach."

"You need cleanin' up anyway," she said decisively. "Come on." She took his arm and started walking, and Britten was too unsteady at the moment to do anything except go along with her.

"Where are you taking me?"

"Back to Grandpappy's wagon. He's got some salve that'll help them cuts and bruises. Might even find some belly tonic."

Britten shook his head, setting off a few fresh waves of pain. "I don't think that's a good idea. Your grandfather doesn't like me."

"He ain't there. He's drunk on his ass in some whore's tent."

"I didn't think you liked me, either," Britten pointed out.

"Never said that." Laura did not look at him, but there was a softness in her voice that he had not heard there before.

When they arrived at Mordecai Vint's wagon, Laura took a cloth and moistened it from their water barrel, then washed the cuts on Britten's face. Her touch was surprisingly gentle. The water stung a bit, but not nearly as much as the salve that she applied next. Britten blinked away involuntary tears as the stinging slowly faded, and when it was gone, his injuries felt surprisingly better.

Laura went into the wagon for a few moments, then came back out to say, "I can't find the tonic. Grandpappy must've drunk it all up."

"That's fine," Britten told her. "I think I'll be all right now. Thank you for helping me."

Laura shrugged and looked away. "Don't like seein' one man 'gainst three. 'Tain't fair."

She was trying to sound cool toward him again, Britten realized, but she was not succeeding too well. He reached out and cupped her chin, tilting her head back so he could see her face. She flinched slightly when he touched her, but she did not try to pull away.

While he looked down at her, he was struck once again by the feeling that under the rough, dirty exterior was something that could be special. With a fingertip he wiped away a smudge on her cheek, and as their eyes looked at each other, he realized that the pain in his middle had faded into a dull ache that he could ignore.

"What the hell is it you really want?" she asked in a voice that was almost a whisper. "Most fellers see something they want, they just grab it. You don't."

"Maybe I don't know what I want," Britten replied slowly. There was a time to ponder questions like that—and a time to say the hell with it.

He brought his mouth down on hers.

Laura stiffened for a moment, then began to respond as Britten's arms went around her, drawing her closer to him. Gone from his mind were any thoughts of trying to get more information about her grandfather. For the moment he was content to hold her, to feel the warmth of her in his embrace, to taste the sweetness of her lips.

When Laura broke the kiss, she rested her head against his shoulder and asked, "Why did you do that?"

"Because I wanted to," Britten said simply.

"That your way of thankin' me?"

"Maybe that's part of it," he said.

She pulled her head back and looked up at him, a fierce expression on her face. "Don't you go toyin' with me," she said. "And don't go thinkin' I'm something I'm not."

"I know. You told me—"

"I told you I ain't no whore. That don't mean I'm some kind o' virgin, neither. You got no idea what it's like to have to get by out here in the middle of nowhere, mister, with nobody but a drunken old sot like Grandpappy to take care of you. I been some places and done some things I ain't too proud of. I've stole and I've lied. I ain't never killed nobody, and I never bedded nobody for money."

"You don't have to say anything else," Britten told her.

"Just don't make me no promises you don't figger to keep."

"All right," Britten said, drawing her back into his embrace. "No promises, Laura. None at all."

That was a good idea, Britten thought, his face turning bleak in the shadows as he stared over her shoulder. He did not want to make any promises . . . not when he might wind up having her grandfather arrested and thrown in jail.

Chapter 9

BRITTEN WAS STIFF AND SORE THE NEXT MORNING, BUT HE was able to get around. When Osgood Newton commented on the halting way the young draftsman was walking, Britten explained, "I took a spill and must have sprained something." He was not sure whether Newton accepted the story.

As far as Britten knew, the beating he had taken was not common knowledge around the camp. The shot had not drawn any attention, and he doubted that the three men who had attacked him would be talking about the incident.

Concentrating on his work was difficult, Britten found as he bent over the maps, the frown on his face reflecting his conflicting emotions. Visions of Laura kept coming into his mind. It was strange how the dirty, unkempt frontier woman was occupying his thoughts with just as much intensity as Deborah Rowland had a week earlier. Nevertheless, his loyalty to Matthew Faraday and the agency demanded that he solve this case and bring the culprit to justice—even if the man turned out to be Mordecai Vint.

Just before noon Newton pulled out his watch,

checked the hour, then snapped the timepiece closed. "You might as well go get something to eat," he said acidly to Britten, who had laid down his pen and was staring thoughtfully at the paper spread out before him. "You're certainly not getting a great deal accomplished around here this morning."

Britten shook his head. "I'm sorry, Mr. Newton. I've got something on my mind."

"Obviously." Newton's voice lost some of its sharp edge. "Go on. Perhaps you'll be more productive this afternoon."

Britten nodded and got up from the big table. He left his coat hanging on the chair, but he did pick up the shell belt and holster he had slung on the back of the chair earlier. Buckling it on, he picked up his hat and went out.

He had just let the tent flap fall shut behind him when he saw an unexpected sight coming down the street toward him—a young woman with long hair the color of corn silk, hair that shone in the sun. She wore a sky-blue cotton dress with white lace around the throat and arms.

"Laura," Britten pronounced involuntarily. He had never seen a more beautiful woman.

She was drawing plenty of attention as she came down the street, and she looked vaguely embarrassed. Most of the men in camp probably did not recognize her, Britten thought. He stepped forward quickly, reaching out to take her arm.

"You look lovely today, Laura," he said, his voice strangely hoarse.

She smiled shyly. "Thank you, Daniel. Reckon I'm right glad you think so. I was a mite worried."

"What in the world about?"

Laura cast her eyes down toward the ground. "I figgered you might think I was silly-lookin'."

Britten shook his head and said, "Hardly. Would you like to have lunch with me?"

"That's why I came lookin' for you." Laura shook her head somewhat wearily. "And to get away from Grandpappy. He don't like the way I look now. Tol' me all that soap was bad for a body."

Britten laughed. He slipped his arm through hers and started toward the dining hall. "Where did you get the dress?" he asked.

"Oh, it's one that Grandpappy had. He was gonna try to sell it to one of them ladies that'll be comin' out here from the East. You reckon it looks good?"

"It looks very good," Britten assured her. He was aware of the eyes following them as they went into the big tent, but he tried to ignore the watchers.

As beautiful as Laura had turned out to be, this development worried Britten. She was going to attract a lot more attention this way. Deborah had drawn her share of lecherous looks since coming to the railhead, but no one was about to bother the betrothed of the construction boss. Laura, being only the granddaughter of a lowly peddler, had no such protection, and the railroad workers would probably regard her as fair game.

Britten could not let that happen. He was going to stay by her side as much as possible.

Over the next several days, Britten put that determination into practice. Laura took her meals with him, and he walked with her to the wagon every night. Old Mordecai was never there, preferring to spend his evenings in the various saloons and brothels, and Britten was worried about Laura spending her nights alone in the wagon. But when he expressed those feelings, she laughed and said, "That big ol' Dragoon takes good care of me at night, Daniel. Ain't nobody gonna bother me while I've got that hogleg close at hand."

Now that Laura had decided not to fight her feelings for him, she told him a great deal about her grandfather and her life with him. It was a grim background, as Britten had supposed, and he was certain that if she were left on her own, she would end up in some crib somewhere, rapidly losing what was left of her youth and vitality.

Nothing she told him about Vint made Britten's suspicions lessen. She admitted that her grandfather had dealt with Indians, although she was not sure what he and the warriors had discussed. The old trader was still a strong suspect, and Britten decided it was time to tell Terence Jennings who he really was and get the construction boss's opinion on the matter.

He came to that conclusion while helping with one of the camp's moves to a new railhead. Since Britten's arrival on the scene, the camp had moved twice, and both times he had been impressed with the speed and efficiency with which a whole tent town could be taken down and transported to a new location. The work began early in the morning, and by late afternoon the camp was six miles farther west, set up and functioning.

When Britten had his own tent pitched and his few belongings stowed away, he strolled over to Jennings's headquarters. The flap of the big tent was down, and Britten pushed it open an inch or so and called, "You in there, Mr. Jennings? It's me, Daniel Britten."

The voice that answered him did not belong to Terence Jennings. "Come in, Daniel," Deborah Rowland called.

Britten swung the flap aside and stepped into the tent, reaching up with his other hand to doff his hat. Deborah was sitting at the large table where Jennings did his paperwork. She wore a lightweight tan blouse with puffed sleeves and a dark green skirt.

She smiled up at him and said, "How nice to see you again, Daniel. If I didn't know better, I'd say you've been avoiding me."

Britten shook his head. "Not at all. I've just been busy with the work."

"And with a certain blond prairie chicken, from what I hear." There was a sharpness in Deborah's tone, and even though she was still smiling, her eyes glittered with a less-than-friendly emotion.

"I've just tried to see that no one bothers Miss Vint," Britten answered uneasily. Dealing with jealous women was not something to which he was accustomed.

"No one bothers *me,*" Deborah pointed out. "Are you saying that Laura Vint is that much more attractive than I am?"

Britten wondered where the hell Jennings was. He had not expected Deborah to be there alone. "That's not what I'm saying at all. No one is going to annoy you, Deborah, not when your father is one of the railroad's major stockholders and your fiancé is the boss of this construction camp."

Deborah shrugged prettily. "I suppose you're right." She stood up and came around the table, moving close to him. "But let's not talk about Laura Vint. Were you looking for Terence, Daniel?"

Britten nodded. "That's right. Do you know where he is?"

Again Deborah shrugged. "Out working somewhere, I suppose. Terence comes and goes as he pleases. That's one of the advantages of authority. Can I do something for you?"

Britten was acutely aware that she was standing only inches away from him, and he felt the compelling power of her eyes as she looked up at him. "I wanted to discuss something with him, but I suppose it can wait."

"If it's something about the railroad, you can tell me. I told you before, I want to know as much as possible about the details of this endeavor."

Britten hesitated. He supposed it would not hurt anything to reveal his true identity to her, since she was Amos Rowland's daughter, after all, but he doubted that it would serve any purpose. Deborah would not know what had been going on in the camp before their arrival. And she had nothing to do with either Callaghan or Vint, so she would not be able to add anything to Britten's theories concerning them.

"I think I'd better wait until I can talk to Mr. Jennings," he said. "I'll come back later. . . ."

He started to turn away, but Deborah stopped him

with a hand on his arm. He felt her thigh brush against his as she said, "I wish you wouldn't go, Daniel. I've missed you."

Abruptly she lifted her face to his, and he tasted the sweet warmth of her mouth as she kissed him. Her fingers tightened on his arm, and her other hand stole up to his neck to caress the back of it. For a moment Britten's arms remained at his side, but then, acting of their own volition, they encircled her, pulling her tightly against him.

The kiss was long and passionate, and Britten could not deny the hunger that grew in him as he held her. A part of his mind thought of Laura Vint and his growing feelings for her, but that small voice was no match for the heat aroused by Deborah's kiss. He was also aware that they were in Terence Jennings's tent and that the construction boss could walk in at any time and catch him kissing Deborah—the woman whom Jennings was going to marry—but he could not stop himself from responding.

Finally Deborah took her lips away from his and whispered, "I told you I had missed you, Daniel. Haven't you missed me?"

"Yes, I have," Britten answered honestly. "But you're engaged to marry another man, remember?"

Deborah slipped out of his embrace and turned away with a pout. "Terence is nice, but he can be so boring at times. All he does is work. Not like you, Daniel."

Britten gave a little laugh. "I'm paid to work, Deborah, just like Jennings. But he's the construction boss. He'll go far in the company. I'm just a draftsman, an assistant at that."

"Perhaps you're right, but you can still do many things that he can't," Deborah said meaningfully.

Britten was casting around for a way to get out of this situation gracefully when the sound of a heavy step outside made him quickly move away from Deborah. The entrance flap was pushed aside, and

Terence Jennings stepped into the tent. He stopped
short when he saw Britten, a puzzled look on his face
as his glance went from Britten to Deborah.

"Hello, Britten," Jennings said with a curt nod. He
moved across the tent to take Deborah into his arms
and gave her a fleeting kiss. Then he turned back to
Britten and said, "Something I can do for you?"

"I asked Daniel to stop by, Terence," Deborah said
quickly.

Britten hesitated. He had intended to tell Jennings
why he was there, but now he was curious why
Deborah would tell a lie. He decided to wait and see
what she had in mind.

Deborah went on. "I asked Daniel to come with us
on our picnic tomorrow, but so far he hasn't given me
an answer."

Picnic? Britten thought. Nothing had been said
about a picnic.

Jennings frowned slightly. "Oh, yes, the picnic. I
still feel funny, Deborah, about taking off in the
middle of the day—I don't think it's good for the
men's morale if the boss flaunts his right to come and
go as he pleases. But I know I promised you, and I'll
abide by that." He relaxed and grinned at Britten.
"Fact is, it might look better if you come along,
Britten. That way, there'll be two men heading out,
and the boys will figure we're combining business with
pleasure. How about it? Are you agreeable, if Osgood
can spare you for an hour or so?"

Britten thought rapidly, then said, "I'm sure it
would be all right. Thank you for the invitation, both
of you. I accept."

He was still curious what Deborah was up to, and
going along with her wishes would be the easiest way
to find out. Besides, if they were away from the
railhead, that would give him the perfect opportunity
to discuss the case with Jennings. In this busy construction camp, there was never any way of being sure
a conversation was not being overheard.

"A little before noon, then," Jennings said. "We'll meet here and then ride out. I'm afraid we can't go far from the camp, though, Deborah. It's too dangerous."

"If you say so, Terence." She turned her dazzling smile on Britten again. "I'll be looking forward to tomorrow, Daniel."

"So will I," Britten said, ducking out of the tent, heading on to the dining hall to get some supper.

Britten had a puzzled frown on his face. Deborah must have felt guilty about nearly being caught in an indiscretion; that was why she had invented the story about inviting him along on the picnic. She obviously still had a strong desire for him.

He was glad Jennings was going to be along on this little jaunt.

That evening, Britten said nothing to Laura about his plans for the next day, telling her only that he would not be around the camp for a while. She made no complaint, but Britten thought he detected a look of disappointment in her eyes.

He did not sleep well that night, and he had a hard time keeping his mind on his work the next morning —an occurrence that was becoming common. Britten thought wryly that it was a good thing being a draftsman for the Kansas Pacific was not his real job; otherwise, he might be worried about his continued employment.

Just before noon he went to Jennings's tent and found Deborah and Jennings waiting for him. Jennings wore his usual work clothes, as did Britten, and both men carried revolvers.

By contrast, Deborah was outfitted in a stylish riding dress, with a smart hat perched on her thick, shining hair. She was lovely, as usual, and Britten could not help but compare her glamour with Laura Vint's homespun appeal. For simple attractiveness, it was hard to decide between the two young women now that Laura had cleaned herself up.

Jennings carried a large wicker basket, which he

strapped on the back of his saddle horse. Two other mounts stood nearby, ready for riders, one of them fitted out with a sidesaddle. Britten wondered where it had come from, then realized Deborah must have brought it with her in the private railroad car.

"Good afternoon, Britten," Jennings said heartily. "We've picked a good day for Deborah's little expedition, don't you think?"

Britten nodded in agreement. "Couldn't be better," he said. Only a few clouds hung in the deep blue sky, and even though the sun beat down warmly, a cooling breeze made things comfortable. He took the reins of the other horse with the standard saddle and swung up.

Jennings helped Deborah into the sidesaddle and mounted up himself. Then the three of them set out, riding northwest from the camp. Britten remembered this part of the territory from his surveying trip with Arbuthnot and the others, but he let Jennings take the lead. The construction boss directed them toward a small hill from which they could look back toward the railhead. A slight ripple in the terrain concealed the camp itself from their view, but they could still hear the ring of hammers as spikes were driven, the whistle of a locomotive as the work train inched forward, and the faint shouts of men. A thin haze of smoke from the engine floated in the air above the camp.

"How's this?" Jennings asked as he reined in at the top of the rise. "Suitable for your picnic, Deborah?"

"Quite suitable," Deborah replied, looking around at the gently rolling terrain.

After the two men had dismounted, Jennings helped Deborah down from the saddle while Britten untied the picnic basket. Delicious aromas floated out from under the cloth covering it. A blanket had also been included, and Britten recognized it as being from the bunk in Deborah's private car, but he knew better than to mention his familiarity with it.

Britten spread the blanket on the grassy top of the

hill, and Deborah sat on it while Jennings began to unpack the food. The last item out of the basket was a bottle of wine.

Sitting there on the colorful blanket in her riding habit, with the breeze making wildflowers sway slightly in the background, Deborah looked pretty enough to have her portrait painted, Britten thought. If he had had any artistic talent, he would have been tempted to undertake the project himself.

The food was simple but good: fried chicken and biscuits, potatoes and beans. Britten drank some of the wine when Jennings poured it into fine crystal glasses brought from Deborah's baggage, but he would rather have had a deep draft of cold creek water.

There was no shade on the hill, and the sun began to get rather warm after they had been there for a while. Britten waited for a chance to speak his piece, and it came when Deborah said, "You look awfully solemn and thoughtful, Daniel. Is something troubling you?"

Britten smiled slightly and reached into his pocket for his pipe and tobacco pouch. Filling the bowl, he said, "I reckon most men would say they didn't have a care in the world if they were sharing a good meal with two friends like you on a day like this. But I do have something on my mind. There's something about me that neither of you knows."

"Oh?" Jennings sounded amused. He was sitting beside Deborah on the blanket, half reclining with his weight on one elbow and the wineglass in his other hand. "And what could that be?"

Britten said flatly, "I'm an agent for Faraday Security Service, sent from Kansas City to investigate your problems with the Indians."

Jennings sat up sharply, wine sloshing from his glass, while Deborah stared openmouthed at Britten. "Let me get this straight," Jennings snapped. "You're a detective?"

Britten was putting the unlit pipe in his mouth as he said, "That's right."

Deborah smiled uncertainly. "You're joking, Daniel. You have to be joking. Detectives are men like . . . well, like Mr. Faraday. Not—"

"Not draftsmen? Not little fellows who look wet behind the ears?" Britten struck a match and put it to the pipe bowl.

Deborah's mouth tightened. "There's no call to be rude, Daniel, just because you took me by surprise with that bit of news."

"Me, too," Jennings added. "Took me by surprise, that is. Why, I had no idea you weren't what you seemed."

"I was just doing my job," Britten said.

Jennings leaned forward, suddenly eager. "What have you found out?" he asked.

Britten took a sip of wine. Both of his companions were gazing raptly at him, as if they were having difficulty believing his claim. He said, "I've found out enough to make me think that you have a traitor in the camp, Jennings. Someone connected with the railroad has sold you out, probably to a group of ranchers and land speculators who want to force the Kansas Pacific to alter its route."

"You have evidence of that?" The question came from Jennings, who seemed to have forgotten what was left of his drink.

Britten shook his head. "Not yet. But I do have a couple of suspects."

"Who?"

"For starters, Sam Callaghan and Mordecai Vint. Both of them stay away from the camp for days at a time, and both of them know the Indians from the old days. You told me yourself that Callaghan is opposed to the building of the railroad. He may think that causing trouble will make building stop, instead of just relocating it."

"What about Vint?"

Britten shrugged. "I know he consorts with Indians and that he wanders where he pleases out here. But that's all I have to go on. Right now, I'd say Callaghan is a much better bet."

Jennings took a bright red neckerchief from the pocket of his pants and wiped sweat off his brow. Britten could understand the gesture. The heat was enough to make a person sweat; also, the things that Britten had just revealed had apparently thrown the construction boss.

"This is incredible," Jennings said. "Just incredible."

"I had hoped to have proof of something by now, but since the Indians have left you alone recently, I haven't had the opportunity."

"That won't last," Jennings said sharply. He stood up and brushed off his pants. "You've given me a lot to think about, Britten. Offhand, I'd say you have good reason to suspect Sam Callaghan. I've had trouble with him right from the first. I thought he was just a stubborn old rounder, but I suppose he'd be capable of selling us out."

"I don't believe any of this," Deborah said sharply. "I certainly don't believe that you're some sort of detective, Daniel. It's absurd."

Britten smiled at her. "Maybe so, but it's the truth, Miss Rowland."

She looked intently at him, as though she was having trouble accepting what he had told them. Britten stepped over to her to help her up. It was plain to see that the picnic was over.

Emptying his pipe of ashes, Britten pocketed it and then held out his hand to Deborah. She took it, and he helped her to her feet. As he lifted her, he looked past her shoulder at the small hills sweeping away to the north, and suddenly his breath seemed to stick in his throat. Riders were approaching.

A whoop went up from the small band of Indians emerging from the scant cover of a rise, and Jennings spun around at the sound. "Dammit!" he barked. "Come on, Deborah!"

Deborah cried out in fear when she saw the Indians galloping toward them. Jennings, grabbing her arm, hurried her to their horses, and the remains of the picnic were forgotten as he all but threw her into the saddle.

"Ride for the railhead!" Jennings snapped as he swatted Deborah's horse on the rump.

Britten, the Starr out and ready, ran to his horse and vaulted into the saddle. By the time he had the animal wheeled around, Jennings had mounted as well. There was a sharp crack and a puff of powder smoke from the band of Indians as one of them fired a rifle.

Britten squeezed off a shot in their direction, but Jennings said, "Forget it! The range is too much for a handgun. Come on. We'll cover Deborah."

The two men kicked their mounts into a gallop, and as they rode hard toward the railhead, Britten saw Deborah about twenty yards ahead of them. They would be able to protect her to a certain extent, since the Indians would have to get through the two of them before they could get their hands on her.

More gunshots came from the pursuing Indians. Though none of the slugs seemed to be coming close, Britten knew the accuracy would improve as the gap closed between them and the warriors.

When the railhead came into sight, Jennings yelled at the top of his lungs and emptied his revolver into the air to alert the workers that trouble was on the way. Britten twisted in his saddle and fired three more shots at the Indians. He was sure that none of his bullets hit anything, but he hoped the shots would at least serve as a distraction.

Jennings poured on the speed, urging his horse to its maximum effort. He pulled up even with Deborah, whose hair had come loose from its elaborate arrangement and was streaming out in the wind. Together they raced past the end of the tracks and circled around behind the locomotive of the work train. The big engine's bulk would provide the best cover for Deborah.

Britten saw the workers running toward him, many of them carrying guns and some even firing past him toward the onrushing Indians. Yanking back on the reins, he hauled his mount to a stop. He dropped out of the saddle and joined the growing line of resistance, jamming more shells into the Starr and then blasting away at the howling savages.

The whistle on the locomotive let out a piercing shriek. Combined with the rattle of gunfire, it let the entire camp know that something was wrong, and more and more men appeared, guns in hand.

Britten saw the warriors suddenly pull their ponies to a halt, most likely deciding that they were up against too many well-armed men for such a small band to fight. With a scattering of shots and defiant, angry whoops, the Indians turned and galloped away, leaving a thin cloud of dust to mark their departure.

A cheer went up from the railroad workers as they saw the Indians' flight, the men waving their rifles in the air and shouting jeers after the Indians. Britten did not waste his breath. He reloaded the Starr again and slid it back in its holster, then hurried around to the other side of the locomotive to look for Jennings and Deborah.

He found them standing together by the engine's cab. Jennings still had his gun out, and Deborah was pale and shaking slightly.

"The Indians have pulled out," Britten told them. "I guess they decided they were outgunned."

Deborah heaved a sigh of relief, letting herself sag slightly against Jennings's brawny form, but the construction boss did not look so relieved. "They'll be back with a lot more braves."

Britten did not reply, but he was afraid Jennings might be right. No matter what had brought it on, the short truce was over.

They were headed into trouble now, real trouble.

Chapter 10

RAIN HAD COME TO KANSAS CITY, CLOAKING THE SKY WITH gray clouds and sending trickles of moisture down the window in Matthew Faraday's office. An appropriate day for being stuck behind a desk, the head of the detective agency thought.

At the sound of a soft knock on the door, Faraday grunted, "Come in." He glanced up as Charles Roth stepped into the office and shut the door behind him. "What is it, Charlie?"

"There's a man out here to see you, Mr. Faraday. He says he's from Washington."

Faraday looked up, his interest growing, and he saw that Roth's face was solemn and serious. "Did he show you his credentials?"

Roth shook his head. "He said he would prefer to talk to you, sir."

Faraday shrugged. "Well, send him in, I suppose. Maybe he'll help liven up the day."

A moment later Roth ushered a tall, distinguished man of middle age into the office. The stranger wore a long gray coat and carried a black top hat in his hands.

135

His brown hair was graying, and he sported a thick mustache and full sideburns.

Faraday extended his hand across the desk. "I'm Matthew Faraday, sir. What can I do for you?"

"My name is Edward Gentry, Mr. Faraday," the man said, shaking the detective's hand. He placed the top hat on a corner of the desk.

"Have a seat, Mr. Gentry." Faraday glanced at Roth and said, "That'll be all, Charlie."

Roth nodded and went out, and Faraday settled himself in the big chair behind the desk. His blue eyes studied the visitor. Gentry looked slightly stuffy, but there was a quick intelligence in the man's gaze as he studied Faraday in return.

"My secretary says you're from Washington," Faraday commented after a moment. "I assume that means the government."

"The highest level of the government, sir," Gentry said.

"The White House?"

When Gentry nodded in affirmation, Faraday lifted an eyebrow and smiled slightly. "It's not often that a representative of the President pays a visit to me, Mr. Gentry. In fact, this is the first time. You won't object if I ask to see some documentation?"

"Not at all." Gentry reached inside his coat and took out an envelope made of thick white paper. As he held it out to Faraday, the detective saw an elaborate seal impressed into the wax that held it closed.

Faraday weighed the heavy envelope in his palm. "It looks authentic enough," he said.

"It is. Do you accept that I am who I say I am, Mr. Faraday?"

"For now . . . yes."

"Then I am authorized to ask you to read the letter inside that envelope, sir."

Carefully Faraday tore open the envelope and took out several sheets of folded paper, and as he unfolded them, he saw that they were indeed official White House stationery. The writing on the paper was a scrawl, but Faraday could make it out. He had plenty of experience reading the hen scratchings of his operatives, he thought wryly as he began to read.

His craggy features became serious as he scanned the words. The missive first introduced Edward Gentry as the personal representative of the President of the United States, then stated that the White House was well aware of Faraday's status as an investigator specializing in work for the railroads. Britten read on:

This office is also cognizant of your independent nature, Mr. Faraday. Therefore, I am requesting of you that your office shall, from time to time, function as an unofficial investigative arm of the executive branch. Certain of us in the government realize that despite the continuing importance of the railroads to the nation's growth, there may be instances when the best interests of the United States will run counter to the best interests of the rail companies. Your job, Mr. Faraday, should you accept it, shall be to balance those interests and ensure that the nation's security and economy are protected. I cannot impress upon you too much the delicate nature of this assignment. . . .

Faraday looked up from the letter, trying to digest the surprising proposition it contained. "You know what this says?" he asked Gentry.

"I do," the man from Washington declared. "And I might add, I believe the President chose the best man for the job when he decided to approach you. Your reputation is excellent."

Faraday quickly read the rest of the letter, which emphasized the need for secrecy, regardless of whether or not he accepted the offer from the White House. At the bottom of the final sheet was the President's signature above the official seal.

Faraday dropped the letter on the desk. He reached up and rubbed his jaw as he pondered what he had read. After a moment he said, "I'm just a detective. I've never worked for the government."

"That's one reason you were selected for this assignment, Mr. Faraday. You have no connection with the President. No one will suspect you of working for him."

"I've always put the interests of my clients first, Mr. Gentry. This letter implies that I might be called on to betray them." Faraday's tone was sharp.

Gentry lifted his narrow shoulders. "I suppose that could happen. In that case you would have to weigh your business ethics against your love for your country."

Faraday's palm slapped the desktop with a crack. "Dammit, man! Don't you understand what you're asking?"

Gentry nodded slowly. "I think I do. And I'm sure the President does."

Faraday stood up abruptly. He turned toward the window and watched the slow, steady drip of the rain. A gray curtain obscured the Missouri River today; he could not even make out the massive structure of the bridge.

When he finally turned around again, he said hollowly, "I accept."

A look of relief flashed across Gentry's face for an instant; then he again became calm and composed. "An excellent decision, sir. I think you will find that things will work out better than you expect."

"I hope so." Faraday's voice was heavy.

Gentry leaned forward. "Since you have accepted the President's proposition, I am now empowered to give you some information about the case your agency is currently investigating."

Faraday frowned. "What the hell do you know about that?"

"You have an agent at the railhead of the Kansas Pacific, I believe, investigating the possibility that someone is deliberately stirring up trouble with the Indians."

Faraday leaned forward, placing his palms flat on the desk. Angrily, he asked, "How the devil do you know that?"

Gentry shook his head with a slight smile. "We have our own sources of information, Mr. Faraday, just as I'm sure you do. What's important is that you need to know your agency is not the first to look into these Indian troubles."

"What do you mean?"

"A government investigator was sent in several weeks ago. We suspect that the Indians are receiving supplies of liquor and guns to keep them in a killing frenzy. Our man was to find out if that was the case and also to discover if someone connected with the rail line was working with the Indians."

Faraday had an idea he knew what Gentry was leading up to as he asked, "What happened to this man of yours?"

"We're not sure," the government man said with a shake of his head. "He made one brief contact, but before we could answer him, the telegraph transmission was interrupted. We never heard from him again."

"He's probably dead," Faraday said flatly.

Gentry nodded. "That's what we presume. However, you have a man on the scene now. Has he been in touch with you?"

Faraday shook his head, frowning again as he thought about Daniel Britten. "I haven't heard anything so far. But that's not unusual. Unless a man needs help or has some positive results to report, I might not hear from him. I've always encouraged my men to rely on their own initiative."

"Can you reach him without compromising his position, perhaps find out if he has made any progress?"

"Possibly." Faraday sat down and clenched his fists. This development put a whole new light on the case. Obviously there was something to Amos Rowland's suspicions about what was happening at the railhead.

And that was where Faraday had sent Daniel Britten—right into the lair of a possible killer.

"I'll be staying here in Kansas City for a while," Gentry said as he stood up. Giving Faraday a card with the name of his hotel, he added, "I'd appreciate it if you'd get in touch with me as soon as you find out anything."

Faraday nodded, and then a calculating look came into his eyes. "One thing you haven't mentioned, Mr. Gentry. How much is the government prepared to pay me for my services and those of my agency?"

Gentry smiled grimly. "I think you'll find that you will be adequately compensated, Mr. Faraday. At the moment that's all I can say on the matter."

"So I'm supposed to just trust you?"

"Surely you don't mind trusting your own government, Mr. Faraday."

Faraday smiled, but there was little humor in the expression. "Of course not. But a government is made up of men, and if I ever find that I'm being double-crossed, I'll come looking for a man—you, sir."

"I think we understand each other." Gentry picked up his top hat. "Good day, Mr. Faraday."

When the man from Washington was gone, Charles Roth came into the inner office and found Faraday staring down at the paperwork scattered on his desk, deep in thought. "Can I do anything for you, sir?" Roth asked.

Faraday shook his head. "I'm sure you're wondering what all that was about, Charlie. I'm afraid I can't tell you right now. Probably the fewer people who know, the better."

"I understand, sir," Roth replied, although Faraday could hear the curiosity in his voice. Eventually the secretary would have to know what was going on, but for the time being Faraday preferred to keep the arrangement with the President to himself.

Faraday's eye fell on a scrap of paper on his desk, and his hand abruptly shot out to pick it up. The paper was the note Britten had sent him from the train station, detailing the robbery attempt by Mose Goreham and a couple of his thugs. The note had been lying on Faraday's desk for over a week now, and he had attached little significance to it since Britten was apparently unhurt by the attack.

But now another possibility suggested itself. Could it be that there had been more to the attack than a simple robbery attempt? If one traitor was inside the Kansas Pacific, it stood to reason that another could be involved.

"Dodd," Faraday said softly to himself. Norman Dodd, Rowland's assistant, had been at that secret meeting at the Rowland mansion. Dodd knew who Britten was, knew that the young agent was going to be leaving Kansas City to go to the railhead. He could have hired Goreham to stage a phony robbery and make sure that Britten wound up dead.

Faraday looked up at Roth. "There is something you can do for me, Charlie," he said. "Get some of our men looking for Mose Goreham. I want to get my hands on that hoodlum so that we can have a nice long talk."

"Yes, sir." Roth nodded. "Is there anything else?"

Faraday stood up and reached for his coat. "Not now. I'm going to pay a visit to Amos Rowland."

Considering the weather, Faraday decided to get his buggy from the livery stable down the street, rather than take his saddle horse. During the drive out to Rowland's house, he pondered what he was going to say to the railroad magnate. He could not reveal what he had learned today from Edward Gentry, but he wanted to know more about Norman Dodd.

Faraday brought the buggy to a stop under the *porte cochere* at the front of the Rowland mansion. Around the flower bed to the left of the entrance was a wrought-iron railing to which Faraday tied the horses. Then he lifted the heavy brass knocker on one of the double doors.

An elderly black man opened the door, and Faraday told the servant, "I'd like to see Mr. Rowland, please. My name is Matthew Faraday."

"Mistuh Rowland is not here at the moment, suh," the man replied in a deep voice.

"Do you know when he'll be back?"

"No, suh, I'm afraid not. He has gone to Chicago on some railroad business."

Faraday bit back a curse. With Rowland out of town, there was a limit as to what he could learn about Dodd. He supposed he could find out where Rowland was staying and wire him, but that might raise too much suspicion on Rowland's part.

"What about Mrs. Rowland?" he asked suddenly. "Could I speak to her, or has she gone to Chicago, too?"

The butler smiled. "Miz Rowland is here, sir. If you'll come in, I'll ask if she will see you."

"Thanks." Faraday stepped inside.

The servant disappeared down a long hall, then came back a moment later to lead Faraday into a parlor. Hester Rowland was standing at a pair of French windows, gazing out at the gloom, her back to Faraday.

The detective held his hat in his hands and said, "Thank you for seeing me, Hester. I really needed to talk to Amos, but perhaps you can help me."

"I'll try, Matthew," she said without turning around. "What is it you need?"

"Did Norman Dodd go to Chicago with Amos?"

Hester shook her head. "Normally he would have, but there were some details here in Kansas City that needed attention. Amos left Mr. Dodd here to take care of them."

Faraday thought he could hear a strange tightness in Hester's voice. He said, "Do you know where I might find Dodd, then?"

"Amos has an office at the Kansas Pacific station. I'm sure that's where Dodd is working."

Faraday nodded. "Thank you, Hester. I want to

have a talk with Dodd." He glanced around the room, wanting to change the subject, and went on. "Where's Deborah today?"

"That's right, you didn't know, did you?"

"Know what?"

"Deborah has gone to the railhead," Hester said. "She's going to be married to the man who's running the construction camp, and she wanted to visit him. Knowing Deborah, she wants to see that everything is being run properly, too."

Faraday frowned. "I'm not one to meddle, Hester, but are you sure it's a good idea to let a young girl go to a place like end-of-track . . .?"

Hester finally turned slightly, but only enough so that Faraday could see the right side of her face. "No, I'm not—but she's headstrong, and I couldn't stop her. But you didn't come just to ask about Deborah, or Amos, or Norman Dodd. What is it, Matthew? Something's wrong, isn't it?"

Faraday stepped forward. "I was about to ask you the same thing. You don't sound like yourself, Hester." He was genuinely concerned about her, but by turning the question around, he also hoped to divert her curiosity.

She swung away from him. "Everything is fine," she insisted. "Why wouldn't it be?"

Faraday gave in to the impulse that gripped him. He reached out, took her arm, and turned her to face him. She resisted at first, then seemed to sag in surrender.

Faraday's features tightened as he saw the large, ugly bruise on the left side of her face. Trenches appeared in his lean cheeks. "My God, Hester!" he exclaimed. "What happened?"

"I—I fell down the stairs." She gave a brittle laugh. "You remember how clumsy I am, Matthew."

"I remember nothing of the sort. You were always the most graceful—"

"Matthew . . . I fell down the stairs." Her voice was quietly insistent.

Faraday took a deep breath. "Of course." He hesitated. "When did Amos leave for Chicago, Hester?"

"Two . . . two days ago."

"When do you expect him back?"

She shook her head. "I don't know. He . . . he didn't say how long he would be gone."

Faraday nodded grimly. "All right. Hester, if you ever need me for anything—"

"I know, Matthew. I know. But everything is fine, really."

He nodded again. "Thanks for the information about Dodd." He turned and walked out of the parlor, his mind spinning.

Amos Rowland had been his friend for a long time, and Faraday did not want to believe that such a man would so abuse his wife. But the evidence had been right in front of his eyes. The timing fit; the bruise on Hester's face looked about two days old.

Faraday untied the horses and pointed the buggy back toward town. Right now he had to keep digging in the case at hand—he owed that to Daniel Britten, whose life might be in deadly danger at this very moment—but when this affair was over, he would get to the bottom of Hester Rowland's problems.

That resolve gripped Matthew Faraday like a hard fist.

Chapter 11

MORDECAI VINT PERCHED ON THE SEAT OF HIS WAGON AS IT lurched across the plains, the trade goods hanging on the sides setting up their usual clatter. As he drove, he kept up a running torrent of curses directed at the mules. The old man was good and angry.

After everything he had done for Laura, the gal had decided she was too good for him. She did not want to come out with him on these trading expeditions anymore. Instead, she preferred to stay behind at the railhead.

"Just wants to make cow eyes at that damned little bastard Britten," Vint muttered under his breath. "Nosy little varmint! Oughta of wrung his neck fer 'im, that's what I shoulda done. . . ."

It was the day after the Indians' abortive raid on the railhead, and Laura had used that as an excuse to ask him not to leave the camp. "Them redskins are probably still out there and lookin' for blood, Grandpappy," she had said to him. "The risk ain't worth it."

Damned little the gal knows about risks, he thought.

When there was money on the line—drinking money and whoring money—any risk was worth it. Vint had heard there was a new ranch up to the northwest, on the edge of the Smoky Hills, and if that was the case, then the hands on the spread might want to buy some of his goods.

Since Vint was in no particular hurry, the wagon moved slowly, not raising much dust with its passage. His sharp eyes scanned the horizon up ahead. He had never been afraid of the Indians, but there was no point in being careless, either. He had fought enough of the savages to know how to avoid them—when he wanted to. Most of the chiefs in the area knew him from the old days and would not harm him. The biggest danger was the chance of running across a band of hotheaded young bucks who might not recognize him. If that happened, they might try to take his scalp.

Vint was not going to worry overmuch about that possibility. When his time was up, it was up. Between now and then, all he cared about was getting his hands on plenty of whiskey and women.

A thin plume of dust spiraled into the blue sky, and when he spotted it, Vint hauled back on the lines and drew his team to a stop. There were several riders, and they were moving fast, he judged. To the east an even smaller bit of haze in the air marked the passage of someone else—a lone rider headed directly toward the larger group.

Vint frowned and ran a hand over his bald, perpetually sunburned scalp. There was something funny about this, something purposeful about the signs. The dust from the larger group was close now, moving from his left to his right. He flicked the reins, getting the mules moving again, and drove the wagon down into a depression in the earth about thirty yards away. He stopped there.

Dropping from the wagon seat, Vint picked up an old Hawken rifle from the floorboard. With the Colt tucked in his belt and the Bowie strapped to his leg, he felt well enough armed to investigate. He started walking, his stubby legs carrying him quickly toward the point where the two dust trails were going to meet.

When the vestiges of his frontiersman's instinct told him that he was close enough, he bellied down on the ground and crawled to the top of a small ridge. Raising his head just enough to see over it, he peered out at a scene that surprised him. There were half a dozen Indians—Sioux, from the looks of them—sitting on their horses and facing a single white man. The white man who sat easily in his saddle, seemingly relaxed in the presence of the warriors, wore a buckskin jacket and had his hat pushed back so that his face was visible in the midday glare.

Mordecai Vint stared in disbelief.

"Gawddamn!" he uttered, the surprised curse not loud enough even to be called a whisper. The voices of the Indians and the white man came clearly to him, even though he was still forty or fifty yards away.

As Vint listened, a stunning realization penetrated his drink-fogged brain. The white man, the man in the buckskin jacket, was responsible for the attacks on the railroad. He was giving the savages orders, by God, and telling them where he had stashed a cache of ammunition for them to pick up!

Vint grimaced, but other than that, he stayed as still as he possibly could. They would kill him if they found him there, he was sure of that.

Finally the white man raised a hand and bade farewell to the braves, then turned his horse and galloped away, back toward the railhead. The Indians rode in the opposite direction, off to start the wheels of their latest devilry in motion.

Mordecai Vint stayed where he was, motionless, for a long time. Sweat trickled down his florid face. When he was fairly certain that everyone had gone, he slid back down the ridge and started to run toward his wagon. When he reached the shabby old vehicle, he hopped up on the seat with an unusual amount of energy. Excitement was coursing through him as he reached into the bed of the wagon and pulled out a half-full bottle. His hand shook slightly as he pulled the cork with his teeth and then tilted the bottle to his lips. The raw whiskey burned all the way down to his stomach, its warmth almost immediately settling his nerves.

When the bottle was empty, he tossed it aside, then lifted his head and looked up. "I'm goin' to be rich!" he told the Kansas sky. "Rich, you hear me!"

He turned the wagon around and started it toward the railhead, laughing all the way.

Laura was surprised to see her grandfather return so soon. When she asked him about his trip to the ranch, Vint brushed the question off. "Couldn't find the place," he said curtly. "Figgered it weren't worth the time an' trouble to hunt it up."

If Laura doubted him, she gave no sign of it. She was too caught up in primping to worry about anything else. Vint settled down in the back of the wagon to wait for nightfall. Once it was dark he could put into effect the plan that had come to him while watching the secret meeting between the white man and the Sioux.

He passed the time by finishing off another bottle. The whiskey, along with the prospect of unexpected wealth, had him basking in a pleasant glow by the time the sun set.

When he judged the time was right, Vint climbed unsteadily out of the wagon and headed for the sprawl of tents that made up the camp. Laura was nowhere around, he realized. She was probably eating supper with Britten. That was good; that way she would not be in his hair—what was left of it.

Vint forced his mind to concentrate on the task at hand. Since most of the tents looked alike, he had to be sure he went to the right one. When he reached it, he saw a lantern burning inside and grinned. The man he wanted to see was there.

Pushing aside the canvas flap over the entrance,

Vint stepped inside, hooked his thumbs in his belt, and waited. The tent's occupant glanced up from the bunk where he was sitting and said in surprise, "What the hell do you want, Vint?"

Vint's smile revealed the brown stubs of his teeth. "Just thought you might like to know I was out northwest of the camp today. Out on the plains."

"So?"

"So a feller can sometimes see things a long ways off that get him a mite curious. A feller might sort of sneak up and take a gander at what's goin' on, quiet-like, you know?"

The man in the tent shook his head. "I don't know what you're talking about."

"The hell you don't, mister. I seen you and them Injuns."

The man came up off the bunk, his hand going toward the holstered gun that lay on the little table close at hand. But before he could reach it, Vint had his Colt pointed toward him.

"Hold it! I figgered you might lose your head. Ain't no need for shootin'. I don't give a damn what you do, mister, but I want my share."

The man stood stiffly, his eyes seeming to measure his chances of drawing his own gun before Vint could blast him. He took a deep breath. "Your share of what?"

"Whatever you're gettin' paid," Vint declared. "And I reckon it's a right pretty sum. You give me, say, a hunnerd dollars, and I ain't goin' to say nothin' about this to nobody."

"A hundred dollars?"

"That's right." Vint nodded.

Again the man took a deep breath. "This is blackmail, Vint. I suppose you know that."

"Don't care what you call it. I just want the money."

"All right," the man said abruptly. "You'll get it. But I don't have that much on me right now. You'll have to give me a little time to gather it up."

"Reckon I can do that."

"Come to the roundhouse later, around ten o'clock. I'll have the cash for you then. Is that all right?"

"Why the roundhouse? Why not back here?"

"Because I don't want you seen around here again, that's why. Hell, it's for your protection as much as mine, Vint."

There was a part of Vint's brain that was crying out for him to be cautious, but it was overwhelmed by the thirst that gripped him. Thirst for whiskey, for women, for the power that money would give him. . . .

"I'll be there," Vint said.

The man in the buckskin jacket was waiting when Vint arrived at the roundhouse at ten o'clock. The old man was punctual, a surprise in someone so slovenly. Money could have quite an effect on a person's behavior, though. The man in the buckskin jacket had good reason to be aware of that.

Vint came out of the shadows near the temporary wooden structure where the work trains were serviced and turned around. The roundhouse was dark and deserted at this time of night, and the nearest tent saloon was at least fifty yards away.

With a smirk on his ugly face, Vint said, "You got that there hunnerd dollars?"

"I've got it," the man replied. "Right here."

Vint came closer, holding out his hand. "I'll take it."

A smile curved the mouth of the man in the buckskin jacket. "Damned right you will."

He brought the knife in his hand up in a smooth, sudden motion, driving the blade into Mordecai Vint's belly.

Daniel Britten was having a drink in one of the saloons when he heard an agonized cry. He had visited several of the saloons thinking that he might find Sam Callaghan, but the big scout did not seem to be around tonight.

Callaghan had not been in camp during the brief Indian attack the day before, either, and that had given Britten plenty to think about.

Now, with the echoes of the scream dying away, Britten dropped his glass and turned toward the entrance of the tent. Several other men had jerked their heads around in the direction of the sound, but none of them seemed to be in a hurry to check on it. Violence was all too common in a hell-on-wheels settlement.

Britten thought there had been something familiar about the sound of the outcry, and hurrying to the entrance of the saloon, he ran out into the night. As far as he could determine, the scream had come from the direction of the roundhouse. He started that way and broke into a run.

As he approached the building, his sharp eyes spotted a shape sprawled on the ground. Britten slipped his gun from its holster as he saw the ominous stillness of the form. Holding the Starr tightly in his hand, he came to a stop next to the body and glanced around, seeing no one else. Behind him several more men had left the saloons and were slowly coming toward him.

Britten's jaw was tight as he knelt beside the silent shape. He saw the buffalo coat and grimaced, knowing that only one man in camp wore such a disreputable garment—Mordecai Vint.

Britten reached out and laid his hand on Vint's back. It came away wet and sticky with the man's blood. But somehow, despite his wounds, the old trader was still alive, and he groaned at Britten's touch.

Moving carefully, Britten grasped Vint's shoulders and rolled him onto his right side. As he did so, the buffalo coat fell open and revealed the huge blood-stain on the trader's filthy shirt. There was not much light there, just the faint glow from distant torches, but Britten could see the dark, spreading blot.

Vint moaned again, and Britten leaned close to him

and asked urgently, "Who did this, Vint? Who did this to you?"

Vint opened his eyes, blinked several times, and stared up uncomprehendingly at Britten. His mouth opened, and with a gust of foul breath, he said, "Should'na trusted him . . . b-buckskinned bastard . . ."

Then his head fell loosely to one side, and Britten knew the old man was dead. Gently, he let Vint's body down on its back.

Some of the other men came up, one of them carrying a torch, its harsh glare illuminating the twisted features of the dead man. Another man took in the massive bloodstain and exclaimed, "Hell, looks like somebody gutted the old goat!"

That was about right, Britten thought grimly of the brutal attack. He stood up, and one of the onlookers asked him, "Did the old man say anything before he died?"

Without thinking, Britten shook his head. "Not a word," he replied. "He was dead when I got here."

Instinct had told him to lie, he realized. No one else had been nearby when Vint breathed his last. No one else knew that his final words had been a clue to his killer's identity.

Or had they? Britten could not be sure of that. Any man so horribly wounded could not be held responsible for what he said. There was a good chance that Vint had not even heard Britten's urgent questions.

"Reckon somebody better find that gal of his and tell her," another man commented.

"I'll do that," Britten said. The thought of breaking the news to Laura sickened him, but it had to be done. He was closer to her than anyone else in camp. No point in postponing the inevitable, he told himself.

Slipping the Starr back in its holster, he turned away as several bystanders moved in to lift the corpse and carry it into the roundhouse. Britten knew that a grave would be dug first thing in the morning.

As he walked toward Vint's wagon, he thought about what had happened. Who was it Vint should not have trusted? Why would anyone want to kill the old man? There could have been several reasons, Britten decided. The killing could have been committed in the course of a simple robbery, but that was unlikely. Everyone around the camp knew that Vint never had much more than two coins to rub together. Any more than that and he would have spent it on liquor.

Britten considered his theory that Vint might have been involved in the effort to delay the railroad and force a change in its route. If that were the case, Vint could have had a partner, and there could have been a falling out between the two men, an argument resulting in murder.

Vint's reference to buckskins was a slim lead at best. Sam Callaghan wore the garments, of course, but it was not unusual to see other men around the camp in buckskins. Britten had even seen Terence Jennings wearing them from time to time.

Still, Vint's dying statement was yet another indication that Sam Callaghan was involved. But was he a killer? That notion gave Britten another sick feeling in the pit of his stomach. He had thought from the first that Callaghan was the most likely suspect, and the respect he had come to feel for the big scout did not change the facts of the case. He resolved to keep a closer eye on the man, since he was the only prime suspect left.

Lost in thought, Britten did not notice he had reached his destination until Laura called to him, "Daniel! Where are you goin'?"

Britten looked up to see that he had walked right past the wagon. Laura had been inside when she called to him, but now she dropped lithely to the ground beside him.

She frowned. "What's wrong, Daniel? You look awful."

Britten took a deep breath and said, "I've got something to tell you, Laura."

She took it better than Britten had expected. Although Laura and her grandfather were still together only because of mutual dependency, she moved into Britten's embrace and sobbed against his chest for several moments when he broke the news. He patted her back somewhat awkwardly. He was not accustomed to comforting grieving women.

"Who would've done such a horrible thing?" she asked with a sniffle.

Britten shook his head. "I don't know. I have a few ideas, but I'm not sure of anything—except that I will find the man responsible for your grandfather's death. That's a promise, Laura."

She shook her head. "Ain't sure I want you to, Daniel. Could be dangerous."

"Don't worry about me. I can take care of myself."

Laura smiled wanly. "That there's what Grandpappy always said."

He held her for a few more minutes, and then she told him that she wanted to be alone for a while.

"I understand," he said quietly, kissing her lightly on the forehead. "If there's anything I can do . . ."

"Reckon not. Not right now. Thanks, Daniel."

He waited until she was back in the wagon, then turned toward the tent where the camp telegrapher slept. The telegraph station was in the same tent, since messages came and went at all hours of the day and night.

The telegrapher, a Western Union employee named Marston, was still awake, though he was occupied at the moment with sending a message for one of the engineers.

"Hello, Britten," the engineer said. "I heard about that old trader being killed and you finding the body. Nasty business, I expect."

"It was." Britten nodded bleakly.

When the telegrapher had finished sending the engineer's wire, Marston looked up at Britten, turned around a pad, and thrust it across his table toward Britten. A stub of pencil was with it. "Write out your message," he said.

Britten picked up the pencil and thoughtfully licked its tip. After a moment he quickly printed a message, ostensibly to his uncle back in Kansas City, inquiring about the health of his seriously ill aunt.

Faraday would be able to read the code at a glance, Britten knew. It was a standard code using certain key words known to all Faraday operatives. When Britten had completed the message, he gave it to Marston, who read it over once, then began working his key with blinding speed. The clicking of the apparatus filled the tent.

"Are you expecting an answer tonight?" Marston asked.

"I don't know," Britten answered honestly. "I suppose it depends on how soon the message reaches my uncle."

Marston nodded. "If one comes in, I know where your tent is. You'll be there?"

"I will."

Britten started back to his tent, wondering if he would hear from Faraday that night. He had decided while talking to Laura that it was time to bring the agency head up to date on what had been happening. This would be the first report Britten had sent in, since he had had nothing concrete to tell his boss before. The situation had changed, however, with the renewed attacks by the Indians and the murder of Mordecai Vint. Things were becoming more serious, Britten sensed. And more deadly . . .

A few minutes after Britten had left the telegrapher's tent, Marston put on his hat and hurried down the street to another tent. In his hand he held the message Britten had written.

When he reached the entrance of the other tent, he called softly, "It's me, Marston."

A muffled voice told him to come in, and as Marston entered, the tent's occupant asked, "What is it?"

"You said you wanted to know if that Britten fellow tried to send any wires." Marston extended the message. "He just wanted to send this one to Kansas City."

The other man took the piece of paper and scanned it, recognizing it to be a coded message without knowing exactly what it meant. A smile creased his face. "You're sure Britten thinks you really sent this?"

"He never noticed that I slipped one of the wires on the key loose," Marston assured him. "He thought it went right on through."

"All right." The other man took a coin out of his pocket and passed it to Marston. "You follow orders very well. Keep it up and you'll be a lot richer than Western Union will ever make you."

Marston grinned. "I'm all for that." He went out, letting the canvas tent flap fall shut behind him.

The tent's owner glanced once more at the message in his hand, then crumpled it into a ball and dropped it into the chimney of the lantern burning on the table. The paper flared up brightly for a moment.

And the glare from the blaze fell on the buckskin jacket lying nearby on the bunk.

Chapter 12

CHARLES ROTH STOPPED SHORT AS HE STEPPED INTO MAT-thew Faraday's office. "Good heavens, sir," he said. "I almost didn't recognize you."

Faraday grinned. He was wearing corduroy pants, a patched jacket, a woolen shirt, and heavy workman's boots. A floppy-brimmed felt hat lay on the desk. Faraday's face was dirty, as were his hands.

"How do I look?" he asked Roth.

"Like . . . like a common laborer," the secretary replied.

"Good!" Faraday exclaimed. "That's exactly what I want to look like."

Roth had become accustomed to his employer's penchant for disguises. "I know from your apparel that you're up to something, sir. I also suspect it's dangerous. Would you mind telling me what it is?"

Faraday picked up several pieces of paper from his desk and held them out to Roth. "These are the reports of the men I assigned to watch Norman Dodd. I've been going over them, and I've noticed that Dodd tends to visit a certain hotel down by the waterfront from time to time. I intend to find out what he's doing there." He stood and picked up the battered hat. "I'm going to follow Dodd and see if he goes to the hotel tonight."

Roth nodded in understanding. "You'll be taking along some of the operatives to assist you, I hope."

Faraday shook his head. "I don't want to draw Dodd's attention. He'll never notice someone like me in that part of town." Settling the hat on his silver hair, Faraday went to the office door and said, "I'll see you tomorrow, Charlie. Why don't you go on home?"

"But, sir—"

Faraday grinned again and went out, ignoring Roth's protest. He knew that the secretary was only concerned about his welfare, but Roth had never been an active part of an investigation. He did not understand that there were times when a man had to go it alone.

As Faraday strode through the streets of Kansas City, his long-legged gait covering ground quickly, he thought about what he and his men had discovered during the last two days. Norman Dodd had been working for Amos Rowland for less than a year, but during that time he had seemingly made himself invaluable to the railroad magnate. Nothing had surfaced about Dodd's career prior to his going to work for Rowland. The man's past was a complete mystery.

Faraday's visit to the Kansas Pacific offices to see Dodd had been fruitless. The man had been polite and helpful on the surface, but he had skillfully turned aside every attempt made by Faraday to learn anything about his background. If Dodd had nothing to hide, Faraday had decided, he would not have had so much practice at evading questions.

Now, after Faraday's agents had devoted several days to shadowing Dodd, only his visits to the Commodore Hotel seemed odd. Faraday's instinct told him that this was the thread he needed to follow.

It was late afternoon, and Faraday stopped for an early supper in a small diner. By the time he was through, the shadows of evening were starting to drop over Kansas City. He was only a block from the Kansas Pacific depot, where Norman Dodd's office was located.

Down the block from the station, Faraday took up a position from where he could keep an eye on the entrance without being noticed. As he waited for Dodd to appear, he wondered if Amos Rowland had returned from his business trip. Hester Rowland's situation had never been out of Faraday's thoughts for long during the past few days. He was worried about her, but there was a limit to what he could do to help her—especially since she did not seem to want his help.

The office workers of the Kansas Pacific were leaving the station when Faraday spotted Norman Dodd. The man walked alone, aloof from the others, as was his manner. According to Faraday's agents, Dodd seemed to have few, if any, friends.

Faraday fell in behind him, keeping a gap of a block between them as Dodd strode briskly to the rooming house where he lived. Faraday lingered down the street, glad that he had stopped earlier for a meal. There was no way of knowing when he would have a chance to eat again.

An hour went by without Dodd's making an appearance. Once during that time Faraday had to duck into an alley when a strolling policeman made his way down the street, but other than that nothing happened.

Full night had fallen by the time Dodd left the rooming house. As the man headed toward the riverfront, Faraday was on his trail again, a grin on his face; it looked as though he was going to have some luck.

The Commodore Hotel, a structure much less imposing than its name, catered to riverboat men, pilgrims on their way west, and the less savory denizens of the waterfront area. The hotel was a two-story building of red brick, and its narrow windows were covered with a thick layer of grime. Dodd went up a short flight of stairs to the entrance and disappeared inside.

Tugging the hat down over his eyes, Faraday walked quickly to the hotel. As he entered the lobby, he spotted Dodd climbing the stairs to the second floor. Faraday's eyes glanced around the small lobby. There was a thin carpet on the floor, two potted plants that were brown and wilted, and a reception desk.

A pair of feet was propped on the desk, and a stentorian snore came from behind the counter. Faraday suppressed a chuckle. The clerk was none too alert, but that did not surprise him.

Moving quietly, Faraday went to the stairs and took them two at a time, landing on the second floor just in time to see a door closing down the hall. The corridor was dimly lit by one lantern on a table at the other end.

No one was in sight. Dodd had to have gone into the room where the door had just closed.

Faraday catfooted his way down the hall. As he paused in front of the door, he saw that at one time the number three had been painted on it. Nearly all of the paint had peeled away from the bare wood, however, leaving only a discoloration shaped like the number.

A soft murmur of voices came from inside the room. Faraday put his ear close to the panel, trying to make out what was being said. He heard two voices, both male. One of them belonged to Norman Dodd; the other was somehow vaguely familiar, but Faraday could not place it.

Though he was able to make out only an occasional word, what he did hear was enough to convince him that he had been right to suspect Norman Dodd: ". . . *railhead* . . . *attack* . . . *savages* . . . *Britten* . . ."

Dodd was selling them out, all right, Faraday thought, and he felt a surge of cold anger at the mention of Daniel Britten. It was hard to keep from bursting in there, but he knew he might be able to do more good by slipping back into the shadows and trying to see whom Dodd was meeting. Slipping his hand underneath the jacket, he made sure the small pistol tucked in his belt was in place and started to turn away from the door.

Suddenly a door across the hall banged open, and two men lunged through it at Faraday. He saw them coming, but before he could pull his gun, the first man had smashed into him, driving Faraday back against the wall. The impact drew a pained grunt from him.

The attacker's arms were almost around the detective in a bear hug when Faraday brought his hands up and smacked his cupped palms over the man's ears. The man howled and jerked back, giving Faraday room to throw a punch at his face.

Even as the first man was rocked back by the blow, the second man tackled Faraday. The detective felt his balance going and fell, taking the second man with him.

Somehow the man got behind him and looped an arm around his neck. Faraday banged an elbow into the man's belly, causing the grip to loosen enough for him to twist around slightly. The maneuver allowed Faraday to drive the heel of his hand up against the man's chin, snapping his head back.

Faraday tore away from him, rolled away a foot or so, and was starting to get to his hands and knees when a boot thudded into his side, spilling him again. But as the first man closed in, trying to kick him again, Faraday lashed out and caught his foot. He shoved hard, upsetting the attacker, and the planks of the floor trembled as the man crashed against them.

Both of his assailants were down now. Faraday seized the opportunity to catapult himself to his feet and yank out his pistol, which somehow had managed to stay in place during the fracas. Leveling it at the two groggy attackers, Faraday rapped, "Hold it!"

A soft footstep sounded behind him, and Faraday started to whirl, but before he could move, a cold ring of metal was pressed to the back of his neck. "Be still and drop the gun," Norman Dodd grated.

Faraday stiffened. He had been too busy to keep track of what was happening in the room where Dodd was having his clandestine meeting. Obviously, the commotion in the hall had attracted the man's attention.

"Be careful with that gun," Faraday said as he let the barrel of his own pistol droop. With the gun hanging from his finger by its trigger guard, he bent slightly and let it fall to the threadbare floor runner.

"Turn around," Dodd commanded. "Slowly."

Faraday did as he was told.

Norman Dodd stared disbelievingly at him. Faraday's hat had been knocked off during the fight, and Dodd recognized him immediately. Looking past Dodd's shoulder, Faraday saw the other man standing in the room's doorway, also holding a pistol and staring at him.

"Faraday!" Edward Gentry exclaimed finally. He lowered his gun. "What are you doing here?"

"That would be a better question for me to ask you," Faraday replied coolly, a slight smile on his rugged face. He looked from Gentry to Dodd, then back again. "What's a presidential adviser doing in a place like this?"

Dodd sighed and looked pained, while Gentry grimaced as he replaced his pistol under his frock coat. "You'd better come in here," Gentry said. "Dodd, I think you should find more efficient helpers."

Dodd glanced disgustedly at the two men who were still sprawled on the floor. "You might as well get out of here," he told them. "You were supposed to stand guard during these meetings, not turn them into a brawl."

One of the men pointed a finger at Faraday. "This son of a bitch was spying on you, Mr. Dodd!" he said indignantly. "We figured you'd want to question him."

"All right, all right," Dodd said wearily. "I'll talk to you later."

The men got to their feet and brushed themselves off, then departed, grumbling. Faraday went into the room with Gentry, and Dodd shut the door behind them.

"Now," said Faraday, "I think someone owes me an explanation."

"Surely you've made some deductions of your own," Gentry replied.

Faraday grunted. "I figure that Dodd must be a government agent, but I haven't had time to go much beyond that."

"That's right," Dodd admitted with a nod. "I've been working for Mr. Gentry all along."

"And you're the one who told him that my agency was working on Rowland's problem with the Indians."

Gentry said, "As I told you, Mr. Faraday, we have our sources of information. We've suspected for quite some time that Rowland was having some unusual difficulties. For the good of the country, we need to get to the bottom of them, no matter who is causing them."

"Like Rowland himself?" Faraday shot back.

Dodd and Gentry both frowned. "You suspect that Rowland may be sabotaging his own railroad?" Dodd asked.

"Perhaps. But if not, someone close to Rowland has sold him out." Faraday quickly told them about the attack on Daniel Britten before the agent even left Kansas City, then said, "I think the traitor did not want Britten going to the railhead to investigate. Only two men knew Britten's real identity, Dodd—you and Rowland. I had decided you were the one, but evidently I was wrong."

"And that leaves only Rowland," Gentry mused.

"That's right," Faraday said with a grim nod. "I don't know why, but it looks like Rowland himself hired those thugs to ambush Britten."

He said nothing about what he had discovered on his last trip to Rowland's house. Amos Rowland had changed greatly in the last few years, Faraday thought. Any man who would mistreat his wife as Rowland apparently had was capable of anything.

Dodd was deep in thought. After a moment, he said, "I suppose it's possible that Rowland has things set up so that he can make more money in the long run by thwarting the Kansas Pacific's progress. If so, he's concealed it well. I've been digging into his business affairs for almost a year now with no sign of wrongdoing on his part."

"He's always been a smart man," Faraday put in. "That's why he came to me and asked me to help him."

Gentry frowned. "I don't understand."

Faraday jerked a thumb at Dodd. "If he suspected that Dodd was a government agent, what better way to throw suspicion off himself than to hire an outsider to investigate the problem? Amos Rowland has always had plenty of confidence. I'm sure he thought he could manage things so that his own tracks were covered."

Gentry smacked a fist into the palm of his other hand, excitement making him lose some of his distinguished air. "Dammit! Faraday, I think you're right! What an incredible plot! But we have no proof, do we?"

Faraday shook his head. "Not yet. I suggest we stop working at cross-purposes and concentrate on finding some." His tone was scathing as he continued. "If you two had trusted me from the first, we could have saved some time."

Dodd flushed angrily. "For all we knew, you were in on the scheme with Rowland or whoever is behind the trouble. We still don't know otherwise."

"Take my word for it," Faraday advised coldly. "I want to get to the bottom of this as much as you gentlemen do. I have a man out there at the railhead who may be in a lot more danger than he realizes."

"All right," Gentry said. "We'll cooperate with you, Faraday. Just don't let us down."

Faraday settled the shabby hat on his head. "And don't get in my way," he said as he went out the door.

The two guards who had jumped him were nowhere to be seen as he left the hotel, but he would not have been surprised to see one or more agents trying to follow him. He had a feeling that Gentry and Dodd did not yet trust him fully.

Hell, he thought wryly, he was not sure he trusted them. But he was going to follow this case through to its conclusion, no matter who got in his way—even a man from Washington.

Faraday expected his office to be closed and dark when he returned, but he found instead that Charles Roth and another man, an agent named Bishop, were waiting for him.

"I'm surprised to see you here, gentlemen," Faraday said as he tossed his hat on the desk. "Trouble?"

Bishop, a tall blond man with a mustache, said, "I got a tip from one of my informants that Mose Goreham and his gang are planning to pull a robbery at Ringgold's place tonight."

Faraday frowned. "Getting brave, isn't he?" Big Art Ringgold ran his gambling palace with an iron hand and was left alone by both the police and his fellow criminals. Faraday knew Ringgold slightly; they had never had occasion to cross swords, but they respected each other.

"I thought if we could nab Goreham in the act, you could maybe find out what you wanted from him," Bishop said.

Faraday pulled the pistol from behind his belt and checked the loads. "Good idea," he said. "Get about four more of the fellows and meet me at Ringgold's. Do you know when Goreham plans to pull the job?"

"Ten o'clock is the word I got."

"Right. Plenty of time." Faraday picked up his hat and walked toward the door.

Roth called after him, "Is there anything I can do, sir?"

Faraday shook his head on the way out. "Go home and get some sleep, Charlie," he said over his shoulder. "With any luck, we're going to be busy tomorrow."

Faraday hurried to the big house near the river where Ringgold's place was located. The man on guard at the door refused to let him in at first, considering the way Faraday was still dressed, but then Art Ringgold himself appeared and said in his booming voice, "Faraday! What the hell are you doing here? Come for a little game of chance?"

"In a manner of speaking," Faraday told the massive, bearded owner of the gambling den. Lowering his voice, he said, "I heard that you're going to be robbed tonight, Ringgold."

Ringgold's frown was like a black thundercloud blotting out the sun. "Who the devil would want to do something like that?" he demanded.

"Let's go to your office," Faraday suggested. "I'll tell you all about it."

Quickly, Faraday told Ringgold about the tip his agent had received. Ringgold splashed whiskey into a couple of glasses and shoved one across the desk.

Faraday concluded, "I've been looking for Goreham for over a week. Now that he's about to surface again, I want him. I've got some questions to ask him."

Ringgold snorted. "I've never had any use for that vicious small-timer. I owe you one for bringing this news to me, Faraday. What can I do to help you?"

Faraday grinned. "I've got a plan."

Big Art Ringgold's office was on the second floor of the house, and it was well known that the massive safe located there sometimes contained tens of thousands of dollars. It would have been a tempting target for thieves—if not for the common knowledge that Ringgold would kill anyone stupid enough to try to rob him, with all the casualness of a man swatting a fly.

But evidently Mose Goreham had plenty of confidence in his own abilities. He and five of his men came into the place a few minutes before ten o'clock, and they immediately ascended the stairs to Ringgold's office, where they found the owner of the gambling house at his desk, scribbling in a large ledger.

"Hello, Art," Goreham said as he sauntered into the office, his men at his back. "Hard at work, I see."

"What do you want, Goreham?" Ringgold asked with a frown. "You know the stakes in my place are too high for your sort."

"Not anymore," Goreham answered. He jerked a gun from under his coat and lined it on Ringgold. "Don't move, Art. We've come for your loot."

Ringgold placed both big hands flat on the desk and leaned back slightly. A huge laugh bellowed up from him. "You damned fools!" he said. "You know you can't get out of here, even if you could make me open the safe. I've got dozens of men downstairs."

"We know that," Goreham replied, keeping his voice cocky. "That's why we're taking you as well as the money."

"You're kidnapping me?" Ringgold asked, disbelief evident in his voice.

"That's the idea."

Suddenly the closet door swung open, and Matthew Faraday stepped out, leveling a revolver at Goreham. "And a damned stupid one it is!" he snapped. "Drop the gun, Goreham!"

Goreham, his eyes showing stunned surprise, jerked his head toward Faraday. He was starting to bring the gun around when Faraday's pistol cracked sharply, and Goreham took a quick step backward, bumping into one of his men. Dropping his pistol, he clutched at his suddenly bloody forearm.

Goreham's men were trying to lift their own guns when the ominous clicking of several revolvers being cocked made them freeze. Faraday's other agents, led by Bishop, crowded into the office, ready to fire.

"My men were planted all over the building,"

Faraday said, "so we had you from the moment you came in. I'd give up if I were you, Mose."

Goreham and his men looked around, despair and fear showing on their faces as they realized how neatly they had been trapped. They were minor criminals, capable enough when the odds were on their side, but they never should have attempted such a foolhardy scheme as the one that had just blown up in their faces.

Ringgold, his face dark with fury, stood up. "Leave Goreham here," he said, "and take the others next door and hold them. That all right with you, Faraday?"

The big detective nodded. "Fine, Art."

Faraday's men herded the gang out of the office after disarming them. Alone now with Faraday and Ringgold, Goreham began to look nervous.

"All right. You caught us," he said. "Go ahead and call the coppers."

Faraday shook his head. "I don't think so, Mose." He stuck his gun behind his belt. "I think we'll just leave you and your men here with Mr. Ringgold. He can do as he sees fit with you."

Goreham's mouth sagged with genuine fear. "You can't do that!" he said shakily. "You're a detective, Faraday. You can't leave us here to be killed!"

Ringgold grinned in satisfaction. "He can do whatever he wants, Goreham. And I like the idea."

Faraday stepped closer to Goreham. "That's exactly what I'm going to do . . . unless you'll answer some questions for me."

Goreham's face was pasty, and his limbs trembled as he said, "What do you want to know?"

"Think back a little over a week," Faraday said. "Were you hired to attack an agent of mine named Daniel Britten while he was on his way to the train station?"

Goreham hesitated, then sighed and nodded. "I might as well admit it, hadn't I? You already know it was me and my lads who done that, don't you?"

"Were you ordered to kill him?"

Goreham shook his head emphatically. "We was to give him a good beatin', cripple him up for a few weeks, but not kill him."

Faraday nodded, a little surprised that whoever was behind the attack would want Britten out of the way for a while but not dead. He did not doubt that Goreham was telling the truth; there was no point now in the man's doing otherwise.

"All right, here's what I really want to know, Goreham. Who hired you to jump Britten?"

Goreham grimaced. "You ain't going to believe me, but I swear it's the truth, Faraday. I don't know. I never saw the lady's face."

Faraday's eyes widened. "Lady? Are you trying to tell me that it was a woman who hired you?"

"I got the word to come to a certain tavern," Goreham said. "I was to go to a room upstairs. There was a curtain there in the room, so that I couldn't see the lady. But I could hear her, right enough. She told me who I was to go after, that I was to make it look like a robbery." Goreham laughed humorlessly. "I figured it was some gal that this Britten fellow had thrown over. A grudge thing, you know?"

Faraday nodded slowly, deep in thought. He knew Daniel Britten fairly well, and he was sure there were no jilted lovers in the young man's past who would pay to have him beaten.

An icy shock raced through Faraday's brain, and he turned to Ringgold and said hoarsely, "You can get him out of here now, Art."

Ringgold frowned. "Do I have to turn him and his men over to the law?"

"I'd appreciate it."

Grumbling, Ringgold herded Goreham out of the office. Faraday could hear his agents ushering the whole gang down the stairs, but his mind was elsewhere. He was remembering the party at Amos Rowland's house and the circumstances of the secret meeting he and Britten had attended.

Briefly, there *had* been someone else at that meeting, someone he had never even considered as a suspect. Deborah Rowland had brought brandy to the men.

Deborah . . . My God! Faraday thought. She could easily have eavesdropped on their conversation, either before or after she brought in the drinks.

And she was at the railhead right now, where Daniel Britten would never suspect her either.

Faraday had no idea why Deborah Rowland would be working against her father, but he was too much of a detective to ignore evidence. He had to get in touch with Britten, to warn him that the other side probably knew exactly who he really was.

He left the gambling house in a hurry, not pausing to explain to Ringgold or Bishop where he was going. There was a telegraph office at the depot, and Faraday was almost running as he covered the several blocks to get there.

He knew the code by heart, as did all his agents. Rapidly, he composed a message to send, telling Britten that his aunt was seriously ill and not expected to live. There were bleak lines on Faraday's face as he handed over the wire and waited while the telegrapher sent it.

A moment later the man looked up at him through the little window in the counter and shook his head. "I'm sorry, sir," he said. "For some reason I can't get through. I'm afraid the railhead doesn't answer."

Chapter 13

FARADAY PUSHED PAST THE BLACK BUTLER AS SOON AS THE man opened the door of the Rowland mansion in answer to the detective's pounding. The butler caught at his arm, but Faraday shook him off. He disliked being rude, but tonight he had no time for manners.

"Where's Mr. Rowland?" Faraday asked as he strode into the foyer.

"Mistuh Rowland ain't here, suh," the butler replied as he hurried after Faraday. "It's awfully late, suh—"

"Yes, it is. How about Mrs. Rowland?"

"I'm here, Matthew," Hester said from the staircase. She was standing a few steps from the top, clutching a silk dressing gown around herself.

Faraday took the steps two at a time, and when he reached Hester, he grasped her hands in his and said earnestly, "I'm sorry to bother you at this hour, Hester, but something very important has come up. Amos isn't here?"

Hester shook her head. "He's back from his trip to Chicago, but I have no idea where he is this evening."

171

Her mouth twisted bitterly. "That's become quite common."

"Do you know if Deborah is still out at the railhead?"

Hester frowned. "Why, I believe so. I swear, that girl is so headstrong. She has no business out there in the wilderness. . . ."

Faraday suspected Deborah did indeed have business at end-of-track. He took a deep breath. "Hester, do you know of any reason why Deborah would want to hurt her father and the Kansas Pacific?"

Hester pulled back, resting a hand on the banister of the stairway. "What?" she asked incredulously. "What in the world do you mean, Matthew?"

Faraday did not answer directly but lifted a hand to touch a new bruise on Hester's cheek. "Did Amos do that?" he asked bluntly.

Hester flinched. "No, I . . . I fell—"

"Dammit! Don't lie to me!" Faraday barked. "We've known each other for too long, and there's no time for lies anymore. Amos beats you, and Deborah knows about it."

Hester's face suddenly crumpled into a mask of pure misery. Tears welled from her eyes as she let herself sag against Faraday. Instinctively, he started to embrace her, but then he stopped himself and put his hands on her shoulders instead, bracing her up so that he could look into her face.

"It's true, isn't it?" he insisted.

"Yes, yes, my God, yes!" Hester wailed. "He's never here anymore, and when he is, he's so angry! I . . . I didn't mind so much when it was just me, but when he started to take it out on Deborah—"

Faraday nodded. He was starting to understand now. Not why Amos Rowland had changed so— probably no one could answer that for sure—but he understood the results of that change.

"Amos drove her away," Hester went on, sobbing. "She was always so . . . so beautiful. . . . You saw her,

Matthew. She discovered that she could get men to do what she wanted, just by using her beauty. And it was always the wrong kind of men, men who used her in return, just like she was using them. . . ." The words had begun to come out in a rush, but now they trailed off.

"I'm sorry it had to come to this, Hester," Faraday said softly.

She lifted her head, her eyes meeting his. "I'm worried about her, Matthew. I don't . . . don't know why she really wanted to go out there on the plains. Could you . . . would you go out there and make sure she's all right? You're the only friend I have left, Matthew."

Faraday nodded. He had planned on catching the first train to the railhead anyway, but there was no need for Hester to know any more about his suspicions. "Of course I will," he said.

"Oh, thank you, Matthew!" Impulsively, Hester threw her arms around Faraday's neck and hugged him tightly.

Looking down over her shoulder, Faraday saw the embarrassed, confused butler standing in the foyer, trying not to stare at them.

Amos Rowland came through the open front door then, and his eyes followed those of the butler. Rowland's face was flushed, and he swayed slightly. His features tightened in fury as he saw Faraday and Hester standing on the stairs, Hester's arms around Faraday's neck and her face pressed against his broad chest.

"I didn't think you were the kind of bastard who would try to steal an old friend's wife, Matthew!" Rowland snapped angrily.

Hester sprang away from Faraday at the sound of her husband's voice, and her hands came up defensively. "Oh! Amos! It . . . it's not what you think, Amos."

"You've been drinking, Amos," Faraday said coldly. "Don't be a fool and make things worse." He started down the stairs toward Rowland.

"A fool, am I?" Rowland shrugged out of the cape that was draped over his shoulders and dropped the gloves that he carried. Reaching up, he took the top hat he wore and tossed it aside. He still grasped his walking stick as he went on. "What the hell am I supposed to think when I come into my own house and see a man pawing my wife—a man I thought was my friend?"

"I was doing nothing of the sort," Faraday replied as he reached the bottom of the steps. "But I think something has happened to the man who used to be *my* friend. I don't know if it's a lust for money or power or both, but you've changed, Amos. And you can't take it out on Hester any longer. I won't allow it. You lay a hand on her again, and you'll answer to me."

"You pious bastard!" Rowland hissed. "You don't know a damned thing about it. Yet you come in here and . . . and . . ." Rowland's rage finally got the best of him. Jerking up his walking stick, he slashed at Faraday with it.

Faraday threw up his left arm to catch the blow, hardly feeling the impact in his anger. Moving so fast that his right fist was a blur, he crashed it into Amos Rowland's face.

Rowland flew backward, past the startled butler. The rail magnate slammed into the wall of the foyer and hung there for a moment, clutching feebly at his bloody nose. Slowly, he slid down to his knees, a high, keening wail of pain coming from his throat.

With a flutter of silk, Hester rushed past Faraday, hurrying to her husband's side. She knelt beside him, sliding an arm around his shoulder to help support him.

Faraday grimaced, though he was not surprised by her action. He would not have expected less from a woman like Hester.

Rowland choked and spat blood from his mouth.

Glaring up at Faraday, he said, "Get out of my house! You're fired, Faraday! You'll never work for the Kansas Pacific again. If I have my way, you'll never work for any railroad again!"

Faraday rubbed the bruised knuckles of his right fist. "I don't think you've got the power to do that, Amos," he said. "But even if you do, I'm not sure it wasn't worth it."

He had turned on his heel and started to stalk out of the mansion when the quick patter of slippered feet stopped him. Hester clutched at his arm. "I'm sorry, Matthew," she said in a low voice, "so sorry this happened. But you promised me about Deborah. . . ."

"I'm leaving tonight," Faraday assured her. "Nothing has changed there. But you should think about some changes, Hester." He looked beyond her to where the butler was slowly helping Rowland to his feet. "You don't have to stay with him, you know."

"I . . . I don't think I'm brave enough to do anything else," Hester said haltingly.

"The woman I once knew was brave enough."

And then he walked out into the night.

Faraday ran along the platform, timing his leap so that he landed on the steps of the train's last car. His strong fingers caught the railing and pulled him up. It had been close; if he had missed this train, he would have had to wait for the next one heading west, fourteen valuable hours in the future.

The conductor appeared in the doorway of the caboose. "What the hell!" he exclaimed as he saw the figure on the rear platform.

Faraday was still in his workingman's disguise, having had no time to change out of it. But he had plenty of cash on him—along with the Navy Colt strapped around his waist. The gun and the money were all he had taken from the office on his fleeting stop there on the way to the station.

"I'm heading west," Faraday said, pressing a bill into the startled conductor's hand. "I'll explain it all later, friend. But right now all I want to do is go get some coffee in the dining car and find a place to sit down. I've got some thinking to do."

Fired by Rowland or not, Faraday was still working for the United States government. The government wanted the railroad going through on schedule, and sometimes the needs of the nation were ignorant of the personalities involved. Besides, Faraday still had an agent out there somewhere in unexpected danger.

He was going to get to the bottom of the trouble plaguing the Kansas Pacific, even if doing so would ultimately benefit Amos Rowland. Matthew Faraday was a detective, and like any good detective—or bloodhound—once he was on the scent, there was nothing to do but go through with the hunt.

Chapter 14

"HELLO, CALLAGHAN," BRITTEN SAID AS HE SIDLED UP TO the plank bar next to the big scout. "Haven't seen you around much lately."

Callaghan tossed off what was left of his drink. "I ain't been around much lately," he replied. "Been mighty busy."

Doing what? Britten wondered.

Britten had been busy himself in the forty-eight hours since Vint had been murdered. The camp had been buzzing about the incident, and it had been easy to draw nearly everyone into conversations about it. So far Britten had not found anyone who would admit to seeing a thing out of the ordinary at the time of the killing, but this was the first time he had been able to catch up to Sam Callaghan.

Britten ordered a drink and then said, "You hear about what happened to old Vint?"

Callaghan nodded. "Messy way to go," he grunted. "I never cared for the smelly old codger, even back in the days when we was both workin' the fur trade, but I wouldn't wish cold steel in the belly on nobody."

"You have any idea why anyone would want to kill him?"

"Reckon somebody coulda got tired of his stink," Callaghan said dryly. "Or figured he cheated 'em. Can't think of nothin' else."

Until now Britten had been careful and subtle in his questioning of the people in the camp, but Callaghan was not the kind of man to respond to subtlety. Bluntly, Britten asked, "Where were you two nights ago, Callaghan?"

Callaghan squinted his left eye and cocked his head. "You askin' me for an alibi, boy?"

"I just wondered what you were doing."

"You sound like some kind of lawman to me. Not that it's any of your business, but I was payin' a visit to one o' them gals over at the Red Slipper. Right feisty, she was. And then yesterday mornin', I rode out on a scoutin' trip. Just got back a half hour or so ago."

Britten nodded. "So you wouldn't know anything about Vint's murder?"

"Just what I've heard since I got back." Callaghan paused. "Boy, I'm really startin' to wonder 'bout you."

Callaghan probably was not the only one, Britten thought. No matter how careful he was, eventually people would start to wonder why he was asking so many questions.

He finished his drink and said, "I've got to go."

Callaghan nodded and turned his attention back to his refilled glass. "Be seein' ya."

Britten left the tent saloon, stopping just outside the entrance to look around the camp. Plenty of torches and lanterns and campfires were burning, giving off light to chase away the darkness. Britten wished he could light a torch and do away with the shadows inside his head, but it was not that simple.

He started toward Terence Jennings's tent. Talking over the case with the construction boss probably would not do any good, but at least he could report his lack of progress to Jennings.

Deborah and Jennings had both cooperated fully with him since he had revealed his true identity to them. They had promised to keep their eyes and ears open in an effort to unearth any clues about Vint's killer, and although it had hardly been necessary, they had even provided alibis of their own for the time of the killing. They had been having a private supper together.

When Britten reached Jennings's tent, he found the construction boss there alone. Deborah had turned in early, Jennings explained. The man was obviously excited about something.

"One of the workers mentioned something interesting to me earlier," Jennings told Britten after waving him to a seat on one of the stools beside the table. "He said he saw Sam Callaghan around the area where Vint was killed, just before the commotion started."

Britten caught his breath. "I just talked to Callaghan. He claims he was over at the Red Slipper at the time."

Jennings snorted. "That's not much of an alibi. He could pay those whores to say anything."

"I agree. But we need some solid evidence before we accuse Callaghan of anything." Britten stood up, the excitement growing inside him as he paced across the tent.

Jennings leaned forward. "Maybe I could go search his tent and turn up something," he suggested.

Britten shook his head. "That's not a bad idea, but it would be better if I did it. I'm not as well known around here as you. Anybody who saw you sneaking around Callaghan's tent would be sure to remember it."

"That's true," Jennings admitted with a thoughtful nod. "You'll need to be careful, though. If Callaghan were to catch you there, he'd probably try to kill you."

Britten grinned. "Callaghan's busy getting drunk. I don't think he'll be going back to his tent anytime soon, but I'll go by the saloon first and make sure he's still putting it away."

Jennings stood up and clasped Britten's arm. "Good luck. This may be the break we need to put an end to the Indian trouble."

Britten had a feeling Jennings was right. Nodding, he pushed out of the tent, heading back toward the saloon he had just left. As he walked through the night, he tried to calm his racing pulse.

Callaghan was still at the bar, Britten saw as he peered through the canvas flap at the saloon's entrance. The big scout was drinking heavily, although the liquor was having no discernible effect on him. Britten knew from experience that Callaghan was probably good for at least another half hour before he would head back to his tent.

Britten ducked into the shadows and began making his way across the camp toward Callaghan's tent. Once he had located it, he crept through the darkness behind it. Then, bellying down on the ground, he lifted the canvas wall and slid swiftly underneath it.

Inside the tent the darkness was almost absolute. Britten waited on the ground for a moment, holding his breath, listening intently to be sure he was alone. When he felt certain he was, he came up on hands and knees and then onto his feet. Slipping his hand into his pocket, he came out with a packet of matches.

Closing his eyes to protect them from the sudden glare, he scratched the lucifer into life on the sole of his boot. A moment later his slitted eyes peered rapidly around the interior of the tent. He was alone, all right.

There was not much in Callaghan's tent, Britten found as he searched quickly. He had to light another match when the first one began to scorch his fingertips. He knelt beside the bunk and pulled out Callaghan's war bag, a large soft leather pouch made of buffalo hide. Inside it Britten could feel a lump.

He opened the drawstring at the neck of the bag, the blood pounding in his head and his gut telling him that he was on the verge of making an important discovery. He reached inside the bag and pulled out a wadded-up garment—a buckskin jacket, just like the one Britten had seen Callaghan wearing a few minutes before in the saloon.

No, this jacket was not exactly the same, Britten suddenly realized. This jacket had a large bloodstain on the sleeve.

His face grim, Britten crumpled the soft buckskin in his fist. This was the piece of evidence he needed to prove Callaghan had killed Mordecai Vint. He still had nothing to indicate that Callaghan and Vint had been working together with the Indians, but with this bit of evidence in his hands, Britten felt confident he could get the truth out of the man.

The flame of the match reached his fingers again, and he hissed and dropped it. No need to light another one now, he thought. All that was left was to slip out of the tent and take the jacket with him. He slid his fingertips along the fabric near the collar and smiled in the darkness, a slightly bitter smile. He had liked Sam Callaghan for a while, but now that the man had been revealed as a killer—

Britten froze, feeling something strange beneath his fingers. After a moment, he dug out another match and lit it. The light revealed what his fingers had felt. Inside the jacket, almost unnoticeable, was a small, unobtrusive tailor's mark, and beside it were several numbers. The mark and the numbers were burned into the buckskin, and Britten recognized the mark as belonging to one of the leading tailors in Kansas City.

Sam Callaghan had never worn this jacket. Britten remembered plainly listening to the old-timer talk about making his own buckskins. Callaghan's feelings about such signs of progress as store-bought clothes were vehement.

But if Callaghan was not the killer, then who was?

Britten let the match die. He stood in the darkness for several long minutes, thinking as hard as he ever had in his life.

* * *

Britten had the buckskin jacket in his hands when he returned to Jennings's tent. "Look at this!" he said triumphantly to the construction boss as he entered.

Jennings stood up, gazing at the jacket with an expectant look on his face. "Is that blood on the sleeve?" he asked.

Britten nodded and said, "I found it in Callaghan's tent, all right. Looks like just what we need to hang him for Vint's murder. From there it's a short step to proving that he and Vint were working together to keep the Indians stirred up. They must have had some sort of falling-out, probably over money."

Jennings clenched a fist. "That bastard!" he exclaimed. "Pretending to be working for us when all along he was trying to ruin the railroad."

"Or at least cause enough trouble to make the Kansas Pacific alter its route." Quickly, Britten explained his theory about the syndicate of ranchers and land speculators.

Jennings nodded in agreement. "We'll get to the bottom of it soon enough, all right." He slapped the butt of his holstered pistol. "Now, what say we go arrest Callaghan? You've got that authority, don't you?"

"Not really, but you do, at least on an unofficial basis. Nobody's going to go against you, Jennings."

"Callaghan might once he realizes we've caught up with him," Jennings said grimly. "He might try to shoot his way out. We'd best be ready for trouble." He took a long stride toward the tent's entrance.

Britten stopped him by saying, "There's just one more little thing I want to do first."

"What's that?"

Britten held up the jacket so that Jennings could see the marks inside the collar. "I want to show you the serial number in this jacket. I'm sure the tailor who made it will be able to tell from his records who bought it. That'll be the last bit of proof we need against Callaghan."

Jennings hesitated, a frown on his face. "Serial number?"

"That's right. First thing in the morning, I'm going to wire my agency in Kansas City and start them tracking down the information."

Jennings stared at him for a moment, and then the construction boss's hand darted toward the Colt holstered on his hip. His fingers had just touched the butt of the gun when Britten dropped the buckskin jacket.

"Hold it!" Britten rapped, leveling the Starr revolver in his hand at Jennings's middle. The jacket had concealed the weapon until now. "Don't make me kill you."

Jennings's face twisted with hatred. "You son of a bitch! You'd never have figured it out if you hadn't found those damned numbers!" His brawny figure trembled with fury, but the rock-steady muzzle of Britten's gun kept him from pulling his Colt.

"That's right," Britten said. "I've been pretty foolish, all right. I let you lead me around by the nose for nearly two weeks, swallowing all the false clues you wanted to feed me. But trying to frame Callaghan for Vint's murder was pushing it too far."

Jennings laughed harshly. "Who the hell's going to believe you? The only evidence you have is that jacket."

"Which I'm going to trace directly back to you through those numbers. And when I asked Vint who killed him, he said with his last breath that his attacker wore buckskins."

"That's no proof of anything," Jennings scoffed.

"Then how long do you think Deborah Rowland is going to lie for you and back up your story when she finds out you're a killer? You've been working to sabotage her father's railroad, working for that syndicate I told you about. The proof's out there, Jennings. All I have to do now is dig it up." Britten's mouth drew back in a humorless smile. "I should have suspected you sooner. You were in a perfect posistion to hurt the road's progress. You know all the plans, you come and go as you please, and no one would ever think to question your movements."

As his voice trailed off, Britten heard the swish of the entrance flap behind him. He stiffened as he heard Deborah gasp, "Daniel! What is this?"

Tightly, Britten said, "You'd better get out of here, Deborah. I've just uncovered some bad news about your intended."

Jennings laughed. "You might make a pretty good detective someday if you get the chance, Britten. But right now you're just a young fool."

Something hard and ominous jabbed into Britten's back before he could reply. Softly, Deborah Rowland said, "I think you'd better drop that gun, Daniel."

Britten stood there for an instant that seemed like an eternity, and then he let the Starr fall to the ground. "You really would shoot me, wouldn't you?" he asked.

"Of course I would. And I'd be sorry about it, too. I like you, Daniel. I really do."

Jennings stepped forward quickly and scooped up the Starr. "If she didn't like you, she wouldn't have slept with you on the train, Britten. But I assure you, Deborah will do whatever is necessary to stop you from ruining things."

Britten stood stock-still except for his head, which he swiveled enough to glance back at Deborah. "You knew all along I was an agent, didn't you?" he asked her.

"That's right, Daniel. I overheard enough of that meeting at Father's party to know what your plan was. But I liked you even then, Daniel. That's why I hired those men to try to keep you from coming out here. I decided I'd rather have you beaten up in Kansas City than killed at the railhead." Deborah sighed and took the gun barrel away from his back while Jennings covered him. "Things just didn't work out."

Britten glanced at the little pistol as she replaced it in her bag. He had no doubt now that she would use it if necessary. He felt a sick sensation in the pit of his stomach. He had learned some hard lessons tonight—although it looked as if he would never have the chance to use them.

But he had to try. Quickly, he said to Deborah, "Did you know that Jennings killed Mordecai Vint? And then he tried to frame Sam Callaghan for the murder."

Deborah glanced at Jennings. "Is that true, Terence? You didn't say anything to me—"

"There was no need to," Jennings cut in. "I did what was necessary, Deborah. Just like you've done what's necessary to pay your father back for what he's done to you and your mother."

Deborah moved toward him, a worried look on her face. "We said there wasn't going to be any killing unless the Indians did it."

"What difference does it make?" Jennings shot back savagely. "Vint's dead, regardless of who did it, and we're safe. He knew I had been meeting with the Indians, Deborah. I had to dispose of him."

Deborah shook her head, obviously shaken by the violence that was hitting home closer than she had expected. By now Britten had guessed that she had been using Jennings to get back at her father for some sort of injury, real or imagined, but he suspected Jennings and the land syndicate had been using her even more.

Urgently, Britten said, "Listen to me, Deborah. You haven't killed anyone yet. You can still get out of this. You can stop Jennings and at least make a start on setting things right."

Deborah hesitated, chewing on her bottom lip, and for an instant Britten thought his words had swayed her. Then a cold hardness settled on her face as she said to Jennings, "Do whatever you have to with him."

Jennings grunted, "I intend to. I'm heading for the Indian camp tonight, and Britten's going with me. They can get rid of him for us."

Deborah nodded. "All right."

"And you're going too."

Her head jerked up. "Why? Why should I go to the Indian camp?"

"Because tomorrow morning at dawn, those savages are going to stage the biggest raid yet. It's going to be a massacre, Deborah, and if you stay here, you could be killed in the fighting. I can only control those heathens to a certain extent."

Deborah took a deep breath. "Will that be the end of it?"

Jennings nodded. "After what happens tomorrow, the Kansas Pacific will have no choice but to alter its route and veer to the north. I'll make a fortune, along with the men I'm really working for."

"I'll go with you," Deborah said hollowly. She had no choice.

Jennings jerked his gun toward the entrance. "Come on, Britten."

Britten hesitated, trying to stall for every second he could. "You were going to make sure Callaghan was killed when we tried to arrest him, weren't you? You knew he'd be drunk, that he'd lose his temper and fight back. Then you'd shoot him to protect yourself and me, and you'd tell everyone in camp that the Indian threat was over since the traitor was dead. They'd really be taken by surprise when the Indians hit at dawn."

"They'll be surprised enough," Jennings snapped. "The business with Callaghan was just a little extra advantage I was trying to get. But the camp will still be wiped out." He lifted the Starr and thumbed back the hammer, lining the barrel on Britten's forehead. "Now move, or I'll kill you right here and make up some story to explain your death. Like you said, who's going to question me?"

He was right, Britten knew. Slowly the three of them moved toward the tent's entrance. Deborah went first, poking her head out and then leaning back in to say, "There's no one around right now."

Jennings prodded Britten in the back with the gun. "Get moving."

Britten stepped out. He had taken only half a dozen steps when fate suddenly played a hand. Around the corner of a nearby tent came Laura Vint. Her face lit up when she spotted Britten, but she looked confused as she saw Deborah Rowland and Terence Jennings— and the gun in Jennings's hand.

"Daniel!" she exclaimed. "What're you—"

"Get her!" Jennings hissed.

As Deborah leaped forward, comprehension seemed to dawn on Laura's face, and her hand flashed to the waistband of the pants she was wearing, in an attempt to draw the pistol she carried there. In the same instant she twisted away and opened her mouth to shout for help.

But Deborah moved with surprising speed and strength, her fist cracking into Laura's jaw, knocking her backward. Deborah yanked her own gun from her bag and lifted it, slashing down at Laura's head with the barrel.

Britten's anger exploded. He whirled with amazing quickness, and even though Jennings had the Starr cocked and ready, Britten was able to knock the barrel aside and then lunge at the construction boss. He drove a fist into Jennings's belly.

The bigger man staggered, but he did not go down. His free hand came around in a looping blow that smashed against the side of Britten's head. Bright lights danced behind the young agent's eyes, and he sensed his equilibrium was failing. As he thudded heavily to the ground, he felt Jennings's knee thump into his back and the Starr dig painfully into the side of his neck.

"Don't move, damn you!" Jennings growled. To Deborah, he snapped, "Tie the girl up! And make sure she's unarmed."

Britten was momentarily stunned by the blow, but then his mind started racing, trying to find a way to get Laura and himself out of this predicament. The only plan he could come up with was a long shot at best, but it was worth a try. He had fallen with his right hand under his body, and sucking in his stomach as far as he could, the fingers of that hand were able to move in the dust. He remained that way, his fingers working, while Deborah searched Laura for weapons, took the gun, and lashed the blond woman's hands together with strips of fabric torn from her own petticoat.

"That won't hold Britten," Jennings said when she was done. "We'll have to take care of him when we get to the corral."

Jennings kept the gun pressed to Britten's head as he ordered the young investigator to his feet. Once Britten was standing, Deborah covered him with her pistol while Jennings hoisted Laura's unconscious form onto his shoulder. With Jennings close behind Britten, the small group made its way to the remuda.

The corral was deserted at this time of night, and at their approach the horses began to mill somewhat nervously. Perhaps they sensed that something out of the ordinary was happening, Britten thought.

"Saddle four horses, Britten," Jennings snapped.

"Four?" Deborah asked, her voice quivering slightly.

"We've got to take the girl with us. She saw us, Deborah. She knows too much."

Again Deborah hesitated, but she had already made one decision that put her over the line. She nodded and said, "All right. Whatever you think is best."

Under the circumstances Britten had little choice but to do as he was told. He picked out four mounts, took saddles from the corral fence, and got the animals ready to ride.

When he was done, Jennings said to Deborah, "Keep your gun on him while I find some rope."

Britten watched Deborah as she pointed her little revolver at him. He could see her features in the moonlight, could see the strain there. But the muzzle of the gun was steady, and she wisely stayed too far away for him to take a chance on jumping her. When Jennings returned carrying a length of rope in his hand and ordered Britten to put his hands behind his back, Britten wearily followed the command.

Jennings was none too gentle, jerking the bonds around Britten's wrists painfully tight. When that was done, he boosted Britten into the saddle of one of the horses, then lifted Laura onto the back of another animal, using a second piece of rope to lash her into the saddle.

"All right," Jennings said when he and Deborah had mounted up as well. "Let's go. And don't try anything, Britten. Once we're away from the camp, I won't hesitate a second to shoot you or your little prairie slut."

"Don't worry," Britten said flatly. "I'll cooperate."

For a while, anyway, he was thinking. That way Laura would stay alive in case help was coming. He had managed to scratch a message into the dirt next to the tent while he was lying on the ground. Now all that had to happen was for someone to see it, understand what it meant, believe it, and ride to the rescue.

Yes, Britten thought bitterly. That was all that had to happen.

Chapter 15

SAM CALLAGHAN HAD LOST TRACK OF HOW MUCH WHISKEY he had put away during the evening. It did not really matter; he had been drinking rotgut since he was a lad of ten. By now his system was used to it.

However much he had consumed, it was not enough to make him so muddled that he did not see the signs of someone having been in his tent. As soon as he scratched a lucifer into life and lit his lantern, he spotted the scuff marks in the dirt next to the tent's rear wall.

Immediately Callaghan's hand went to the big pistol on his hip. He tensed, ready for trouble, as his eyes adjusted to the glare of the lantern. When he saw that no one was there waiting to ambush him, he relaxed slightly.

"Now who the Sam Hill'd be pokin' around in here?" he muttered to himself. To his experienced eyes the story was plain—someone had crawled into his tent, searched it, then crawled out again.

Callaghan spotted his war bag lying next to the bunk. It had been opened, but as he scooped it up and checked its contents, he decided that nothing was missing. All the pouch contained was a few odds and ends, a spare pipe, an elk's tooth, a tin of matches, and a cracked mirror.

Picking up the lantern, Callaghan left the tent and circled around to the back. He immediately spotted the trail leading away, and as he followed the tracks, the big scout wore his usual squint.

The trail led to a tent Callaghan recognized as belonging to Terence Jennings. Callaghan's frown of puzzlement deepened. *Why would Jennings be sneaking around his tent?* he wondered. Stepping to the entrance, Callaghan roared, "You in there, Jennings?"

When no reply came from inside, Callaghan shook his head and rubbed his grizzled jaw. He pushed the canvas flap aside and peered into the tent. No one was there, he realized, and he started to turn away.

Then out of the corner of his eye he saw something that puzzled him even more. Looking closer, he saw that sticking out from under Jennings's bunk was the sleeve of a buckskin jacket. Callaghan stepped into the tent and bent over to snag the jacket, which from the looks of it had been kicked underneath the bunk. As he pulled it out, he saw the reddish-brown stain on the other sleeve.

He had seen enough blood in his day to recognize it immediately. Somebody had bled like a stuck pig on the arm of the man wearing this jacket.

Callaghan had developed an instinct for trouble over the years, and alarms were going off in his head as he stepped back outside and took a closer look at the ground around the tent. Sure enough, he found the signs of a struggle. And mixed in with the marks was something else.

"Gawddamn!" Callaghan exclaimed as he leaned over and shone the light on the scribbling in the dirt. The letters wavered and trailed off, but the message they conveyed was clear enough: *Taken to Indian camp. Britten.*

Callaghan cursed again. What the devil was Britten up to? He was in trouble, that much was obvious, and Callaghan sort of liked the little fellow. It was up to him to go yank Britten out of whatever mess he had gotten into.

Callaghan knew from his scouting trips that the Sioux and the Cheyenne had been gathering up to the north, on the edge of the hills. Even though things had been pretty quiet lately, he also knew the peace would not last. He had planned on warning Jennings that a big attack was coming, and now he went in search of the construction boss to let him know Britten had been kidnapped.

Moving quickly through the camp, Callaghan asked around for Jennings and after fifteen minutes or so came to the conclusion that the man was nowhere around. That was strange, he thought. Jennings did not usually leave the camp at night.

Callaghan knew he could not afford to waste much more time if he was going to rescue Britten. Ducking into a couple of saloons, he enlisted the aid of a handful of his friends, all of them salty hombres who were more than pleased by the prospect of raiding an Indian camp to rescue a captive white man.

Callaghan and his five companions had just turned toward the remuda when the whistle of an arriving train drew the scout's attention. He glanced at one of his friends, a surveyor named Mundy, and said, said, "Didn't know there was a train comin' in tonight."

Mundy was frowning. "Wasn't supposed to be. We'd better go over there and see what's going on, Sam."

Callaghan considered the proposition for a few seconds, then nodded. He and the others headed for the newly built station.

The locomotive was hissing to a stop beside the platform as the group of men arrived. Callaghan saw that it was pulling a work train, but the flatcars were not loaded, nor did there seem to be any passengers riding on them.

A tall man stepped down from the cab of the engine. He was hatless, and moonlight shone on his silvery hair. There was a gun in his hand.

The driver stood in the cab and pointed a finger at the man as Callaghan and the others hurried up. "Grab him!" the driver shouted angrily. "He's a crazy man! He made me come out here at gunpoint!"

The man tilted the barrel of his Colt toward Callaghan and his companions, stopping them in their tracks. He grinned slightly, but he was obviously ready to use the gun if he had to. "Just take it easy, gents," he said quietly but firmly. "I don't want any trouble. I'm just looking for a man called Daniel Britten."

"What the hell!" Callaghan exclaimed. "We was just goin' after Britten our ownselves. Seems like somebody carted him off to an Injun camp north of here." The big man frowned menacingly. "That gun don't scare me much, mister. I can take a few slugs and still get my hands 'round your neck. Now, just who the hell are you?"

The man said, "My name is Matthew Faraday."

Britten had never known the depth of despair that he felt as they rode toward the Indian camp. He realized what a slim chance there was that any help would be forthcoming from the railhead. Before the night was over, he would probably be dead. Laura would die, too, and so would dozens of men at the railhead when the Indians attacked.

Laura had regained consciousness when they were several miles away from end-of-track, and the stream of profanity that erupted from her surprised even Britten. Being hit over the head and knocked out had made her forget the effort she had been making to be more civilized. Old Mordecai would have been proud of her cussing, Britten thought.

The group stopped long enough for Jennings to cut Laura loose and allow her to sit upright in her saddle. He then reinforced the bindings Deborah had placed on the woman's wrists with some cords from his saddlebag, and the four of them started north again.

There was little conversation among them, so Deborah was breaking a long silence when she said to Jennings, "Do the savages have to wipe out the whole camp, Terence? Wouldn't a quick raid do just as well?"

Jennings shook his head. "I've been holding them back too long as it is, Deborah. Besides, the Kansas Pacific builders have to realize that they'll pay too high a price if they persist in following the current route." His mouth stretched in a grin. "What are a couple of hundred dumb laborers compared to the money we'll make off this deal?"

Britten glanced over at Deborah and saw a shudder run through her. He did not know everything that was behind her betrayal of her father, but she was obviously torn by her conflicting emotions. She did not want the blood of so many innocent men on her conscience . . . but Deborah Rowland, who apparently was used to wrapping men around her little finger, had finally run up against someone more ruthless.

While Jennings was talking, Britten decided to take advantage of the opportunity to ask him a question. He said, "That Indian raid we had to run away from after the picnic—you staged that for my benefit, didn't you, Jennings?"

The construction boss laughed. "You have to admit, Britten, you sure as hell didn't suspect me after that."

Britten shrugged. Jennings was right.

Nothing else was said during the ride. Pinpoints of light appeared on the horizon ahead of them and grew into the campfires of the Indians as the riders approached. When they were near the camp, Britten caught his breath. The circle of fires was huge; this had to be the largest band of warriors he had ever run across.

Indians appeared out of the darkness on both sides of them, riding along as escorts. Jennings led the group right into the heart of the camp, pulling his

horse to a halt in front of a wizened old chief wearing
an impressive headdress. Jennings spoke briefly in the
Sioux tongue, and while Britten could not understand
all that was said, he recognized the words as a
greeting.

Deborah and Laura were both pale in the firelight,
plainly frightened to be surrounded by hundreds of
Indians. Deborah got down from her saddle by herself, and then several braves hurried forward to haul
down the captives. Jennings was explaining in English
now to the chief that the two prisoners knew of the
impending raid and had to be killed.

The chief nodded solemnly. "It shall be done," he
promised. "The woman would make a good wife for
one of my warriors, however."

Jennings shook his head. "I'm sorry, Soaring Hawk,
but it is my thinking that both should be killed—just
to make sure that nothing interferes with tomorrow's
great victory over the white men and the iron horse."

Soaring Hawk's narrow old shoulders lifted as he
said, "As you wish."

Jennings came over to where Britten, Laura, and
Deborah stood. Deborah was staying close to the
prisoners, as if the nearness of other whites was
reassuring to her. Jennings smiled cockily at Britten
and said, "I guess I'll be leaving you and your friend
here with the chief and his men, Britten. Sorry you
won't get to see the end of this."

"What about you?" Britten asked, trying to keep his
mind off what was going to happen. "Are you and
Deborah staying?"

Jennings shook his head. "I don't think that would
be a good idea." He lowered his voice. "These redskins will be working themselves up all night, and it
wouldn't be wise to tempt them with a couple of extra
scalps. No, Deborah and I will head back toward the
railhead and lie low not far from it. Then, after the
massacre tomorrow morning, we can slip back in and
pretend to be the sole survivors. Our tracks will be
covered."

"Not forever," Britten snapped, his tightly controlled anger finally surfacing. "Someday someone will find out what you've done, Jennings, and then you'll pay for it."

"I don't think so. Besides, I'll be too rich by then to give a damn who finds out."

With a chuckle Jennings reached out, grasped Deborah's arm, and pulled her toward the horses. Deborah cast a glance over her shoulder at Britten, and it was the most hopeless look he had ever seen. She climbed onto her horse, then rode out of the camp at Jennings's side.

"That bitch," Laura said coldly. "Reckon I'd like to take my Bowie and do some carvin' on that lily-white skin of her'n."

"That wouldn't do any good," Britten said. "Jennings is the one who's really responsible for this."

Laura shrank against him as the circle of savages around them began to close in. Britten wished he could put his arms around her, hold her, comfort her as much as possible before the end came. But he could not even do that.

There was nothing he could do. Nothing . . .

Sam Callaghan and Matthew Faraday lay belly-down on a slight rise that gave them a view of the Indian camp. The fires below provided plenty of illumination for the awful scene that met their eyes.

Callaghan's hard hand on Faraday's shoulder held the detective down. "Rest easy," the big scout hissed. "We'll get 'em outta there."

"When?" Faraday asked. "When they've stripped all the skin off Britten?"

It had taken only a few minutes for Faraday and Callaghan to understand each other back at the railhead. When both men put together their knowledge of the situation, the picture they had was still incomplete, but enough of it made sense for them to realize that Britten was in bad trouble. Faraday had joined the group of rescuers, and they had left the railhead quickly, stopping only for a moment at one of the storage sheds, where Callaghan ducked inside, then came back out again without offering any explanation.

They rode hard out on the plains, slowing only when they neared the vicinity of the Indian encampment. Then Callaghan ordered that they proceed on foot.

Now the camp was only a hundred yards distant, and the men were close enough to see the Indians torturing the staked-out Daniel Britten.

Britten's chest was covered with blood, and for an awful moment at first, Faraday thought he was already dead. But then the young agent's head moved, and his shoulders thrashed as another brave moved in wielding a sharp knife.

"Right now it looks a lot worse'n it really is," Callaghan cautioned. "They're peelin' a little hide off, makin' a whole passel of cuts and scratches. This is just to start things off. The real fun ain't started yet."

"What about the girl?" Faraday asked. Seeing Laura Vint staked out near Britten had come as another shock, since none of them had known that the Indians also had taken a female prisoner.

Callaghan shook his head. "They won't take near as long to kill her. Them bucks'll work themselves up torturin' Britten, then let some of it off by molestin' the gal. After an hour or so, she won't be dead, but her mind'll be gone. Won't be fun for them heathens after that, so they'll just slit her throat and be done with it."

Faraday's fist tightened on the Colt he held. Between clenched teeth, he said, "What do you suggest we do, Mr. Callaghan?"

"Well, sir, we're a mite outnumbered." He patted the Henry rifle on the ground beside him. "Smartest thing to do'd be to put a couple of slugs in them young folks and then sort of fade out of here, fast-like. But I reckon you don't much care for that idea."

Faraday shook his head. "No. I don't."

Callaghan sighed. "Then I s'pose we got to go down

yonder and get 'em out." He turned his head and spoke to the other men gazing down at the Indian camp. "That all right with you boys?"

Grunts of assent came back rapidly.

Callaghan issued the orders. He spread the men out along the ridge, putting a good distance between each of them. "You 'n' me'll go down there and try to get 'em loose," he said to Faraday. "The boys up here'll make it look and sound like we got plenty of men. They'll give us coverin' fire. Got to tell you, though, Mr. Faraday, there's a good chance we won't be comin' back up the hill."

"I know that," Faraday said calmly. "But Britten is my man, and that young woman is just an innocent victim."

Callaghan checked the loads in his Dragoon, then shoved the big pistol back in its holster. "Well, hell, let's go," he said.

Faraday followed the big man's lead, stepping where he stepped, pausing when he paused. They moved in almost complete silence and within fifteen minutes were on the edge of the Indian camp. Their pace slowed even more, as Callaghan kept an eye out for sentries and dogs.

Crouching behind a tepee, Callaghan held out a hand to stop Faraday, then put his mouth close to the detective's ear. "How are you at throwin' things?" he asked in a whisper.

Faraday frowned. "All right, I suppose," he hissed back. "Why?"

Callaghan reached under his buckskin jacket and pulled out a small pouch. "Reckon you could heave this here blastin' powder in that campfire over there?"

A grin broke out on Faraday's face as he took the little bag. He nodded without saying anything, and Callaghan motioned for him to move over behind another tepee. Faraday slid across the open space, moving quickly and silently. When he was in position, he nodded again to Callaghan.

The scout drew out his pistol, pulled the hammer

back, and gave Faraday a lopsided grin. Then he surged up, coming out from behind the tepee with a howl. The Dragoon blasted, the slug tearing a fist-sized hole through a brave twenty feet away.

Faraday stood up and hurled the bag of blasting powder into the nearest campfire. He threw himself to the side as the explosive went up with a blast that shook the earth under him. Then he was on his feet, too, running into the middle of the camp and triggering the Colt at the shocked Indians. From the top of the ridge, rifles began to crack.

Powder smoke drifted in front of Faraday's face. He could not see for a moment, but he kept firing as he ran forward. Then he jerked to a stop as he almost tripped over Daniel Britten's staked-out body.

Britten stared up at him with wide eyes, surprise overwhelming the pain he had to be feeling. The agent's bare chest was a hideous sight, but his face was still etched in lines of defiance. Faraday yanked his knife from its sheath and slashed at the cords holding Britten.

As soon as Britten's hands were free, he sat up, finding the strength somewhere to snatch the knife from Faraday and begin cutting the bonds on his legs. Faraday twisted, still kneeling, and fired at a brave who was leaping toward them with a knife upraised. The bullet punched through the Indian's throat, spilling him in his own blood.

Free now, Britten rolled to the side, lunging toward Laura, who whimpered in fear as he cut her ropes. Her urgent shriek warned Britten to whirl around as the last bonds holding her fell away. The knife left his hand and flickered through the night to plunge into the chest of a warrior who was aiming a rifle at them. The Indian staggered back, dropping the weapon, and fell with his fingers clutched futilely around the knife's handle.

Britten sprang toward the fallen carbine, snatching it up and blasting away at the horde of Indians, working the lever with blinding speed. He had no idea where he was getting the strength and stamina to be fighting back, but there was no time to think about that.

Faraday ran to Laura Vint's side and grasped her arm, hauling her to her feet. "Can you run?" he asked her. When she nodded, he pointed toward the rise. "Move! There are men up there to help you!"

Laura broke into a desperate run, heading for a gap between two tepees and starting up the hill. A steady stream of rifle fire poured down over her head, many of the shots knocking Indians off their feet.

Faraday looked around wildly, spotted Britten using a rifle, and saw Callaghan nearby wielding the empty Dragoon as a club in one hand and slashing with the Bowie in the other. Callaghan suddenly bulled his way out of the knot of struggling men around him and dashed toward the rope corral at the edge of the camp where the Indian ponies were kept.

Britten and Faraday both saw what Callaghan was doing and gave him a withering rain of covering fire. The scout's broad blade sliced through the ropes of the corral, and the frightened horses burst out, running wild-eyed through the camp. Callaghan dodged aside with uncommon grace for such a big man, grasping the mane of one of the hardy little ponies and swinging onto its back. He rode toward Faraday and Britten, forcing a couple of the horses to veer toward the white men as well.

The camp was in complete disarray by now. The Indians must have thought there were fifty men up on the ridge, judging by the devastating effects of their volleys. The explosion had started the confusion, and everything else had just increased it. Now, as Faraday and Britten awkwardly leaped onto the horses, the white men were able to gallop out of the camp with no immediate pursuit.

Faraday spotted Laura running up the rise and pointed her out to Callaghan. The scout angled toward her, barely slowing as he raced by her. He leaned over slightly, his long arm shooting out, and in the next instant Laura was perched on the back of the pony with him, held there by his iron grip.

By the time they reached the top of the hill, the other men in the rescue party were mounted and ready to ride. Callaghan waved them on, and together the entire group pounded south.

Britten and Faraday were both accustomed to saddles, and the detectives were forced to hang on for dear life to the manes of their spirited mounts. But Britten was able to move his horse close enough to Faraday's to shout, "The Indians are going to attack the camp at the railhead at dawn!"

Faraday glanced at the eastern sky. It was slowly turning gray now. In another hour or so, the sun would appear. Faraday looked back. He could not see far behind them in the darkness, but he knew without seeing it that a huge cloud of dust was boiling up there. The Indians would be hot on the trail of their escaped captives, and that pursuit would ultimately end at the railhead. If the savages already had an attack planned, they would surely carry through with it now.

"We have to warn the camp!" Faraday shouted back. He wished he knew what had been happening since Britten arrived at end-of-track. Callaghan had said that Terence Jennings, the construction boss, had disappeared, too. And where was Deborah Rowland? He had promised Hester that he would find her and make certain that she was all right. Now she might be facing the same bloody fate as everyone else at the railhead.

But there would be time enough for questions and answers later, Faraday thought grimly. Everything could be sorted out after the sun came up.

If they were still alive . . .

Chapter 16

THE SURGE OF STRENGTH THAT BRITTEN HAD EXPERIENCED at the time of the rescue began to wear off during the desperate chase back to the railhead. He had lost too much blood, had endured too much pain. As he leaned forward over the neck of the Indian pony, he had to grit his teeth and hang on tightly with each jarring hoofbeat.

But as the sky lightened in the east, the hope that they might be in time to alert the railroad camp began to grow in him, revitalizing him to a certain extent. Faraday and Callaghan could carry on now if something happened to him, but the desire to be in on the finish gave him new energy.

As the lights of the railhead came into view, Sam Callaghan let out a whoop. "There she is!" he shouted. "Ride like the devil, men!"

That last mile seemed to take forever to cover. Faintly, Britten heard angry cries behind them, war whoops, and the pounding of many, many hooves. The Indians were close.

Callaghan steered his horse with his knees as he

kept one arm around Laura and used the other to yank out his pistol. He discharged the weapon in the air, shouting at the top of his lungs as he did so, and the other men followed his example. No matter how sleepy or how drunk the men in the camp were, they would hear the approach of these shooting, howling banshees.

Britten saw men pouring out of the tents, carrying rifles and handguns and lanterns. A few of them lifted their weapons and started to fire, but they were stopped by other men who heard the scout yelling, "It's Callaghan! Don't shoot! Indians a half mile back!"

Callaghan repeated the message as he led the group of riders around the edge of the camp. Britten swayed on the back of the pony as they galloped behind the relative shelter of the work train. Vaguely, he wondered what it was doing there; the next work train was not scheduled to arrive until later in the morning.

Hauling his horse to a stop, Callaghan dropped out of the saddle, taking Laura with him. Faraday's booted feet hit the ground a second later, and the detective looked around for Britten. The other men in the rescue party were leaping off their horses and racing toward the other side of the camp, where the Indians would be attacking within moments.

Britten tried to halt the skittish pony, but his strength deserted him just long enough for his fingers to slip from the mane. He felt himself starting to fall—

Then Matthew Faraday's strong hands caught him, lowering him gently to the ground. "You'll be all right, son," Faraday told him. "Let's get you to a doctor."

Callaghan appeared beside the detective. "I'll show you where the sawbones's tent is," he rumbled. Laura was still leaning on him. "The doc needs to look at both these younkers."

Britten heard the crackle of rifle fire from the other side of the camp. Looking up, he saw more men standing on the flatcars of the work train, firing off to the north. Mixed in with the explosions of guns were the shrill cries of the attacking Indians.

He wanted to be part of the camp's defense, but his legs did not seem to want to work. Faraday half carried him toward the camp doctor's tent, following Callaghan, who was carrying Laura in similar fashion. When they got to the tent, the middle-aged, gray-haired doctor was just coming out with his bag clutched in his hand.

"Got your first customers right here, Doc," Callaghan said.

The physician glanced at Britten's bare, bloody chest, then asked, "My God! What happened to this man?"

"Injuns," Callaghan replied simply. "The gal may be hurt some, too."

"Take them into the tent," the doctor ordered briskly.

Faraday and Callaghan carried the two people inside. Britten felt himself being lowered onto a cot, and then strong but gentle hands were cleaning away the dried blood on his chest. Pain welled up inside him, rolling through him like a wave that carried him off into the darkness. He never saw the rays of sunlight that suddenly slanted into the tent as the sun rose.

A mile to the west of the camp, Terence Jennings squinted into the sun through the field glasses he held to his eyes. "Dammit!" he said bitterly. "Something must have warned them. It looks like they were ready for the attack."

Deborah sat on her horse beside him, her face still pale and drawn. "There was a lot of shooting and yelling. Do you think Daniel could have gotten away and come to alert the camp?"

"No," Jennings snapped. "No chance. I'm sorry, Deborah, but your little friend is dead by now." His voice was cold and harsh.

Deborah stared at him for a long moment, then said, "I don't think I ever really knew you."

Jennings lowered the field glasses and smiled humorlessly at her. "No, I don't think you did. But I'm all you have now, aren't I?"

She did not bother to deny it.

They watched while the attack ran its course. Although the Indians had the railroad workers outnumbered, there were more rifles in the camp and more men who were skilled in the use of their weapons. Jennings's face grew increasingly bitter as it became obvious that the raid would fail.

That was exactly what happened. Less than an hour after dawn, the Indians pulled back out of rifle range, howled, shook their rifles and bows at the white men in futile rage, then wheeled their ponies and galloped away to the north, leaving only a thin cloud of dust to mark their retreat. They took their dead with them.

Jennings took off his hat, brushed his hair back, and ran a hand over his face as he drew a deep breath. "We might as well go back," he said, his voice tightly controlled. "We'll slip into camp. With all of the confusion, maybe no one will have noticed that we weren't there during the attack." He squared his shoulders. "There'll be other times. We'll win yet."

Nodding miserably, Deborah started her horse into motion, following Jennings back toward the scene of the battle.

Callaghan and Faraday stood side by side behind an overturned wagon, firing a couple of final shots at the departing Indians. They had fought like this all through the raid, Callaghan using his Henry, Faraday a borrowed rifle. Together, they had accounted for quite a few of the dead attackers, and now, as they turned toward each other, each man's smoke-grimed face broke into a grin.

"Not a bad scrape," Callaghan said.

"It'll do," Faraday replied.

Callaghan spat and cradled the Henry in his big arms. "Let's go see how Britten and the Vint gal is doin'," he suggested.

Faraday fell in step beside the scout as they made

their way through the camp toward the doctor's tent. Men were hurrying everywhere, some to check on injuries, some to form a line of guards on the camp's perimeter on the slim chance that the Indians might regroup and come back.

Britten was coming out of the doctor's tent when Faraday and Callaghan got there. From somewhere the young agent had gotten a gun belt and strapped it on; a Colt rode in the holster. Wide strips of bandages were wrapped tightly around his torso, and a borrowed shirt was draped over his shoulders.

Laura Vint came out of the tent behind him. She clutched at his arm and said urgently, "I tell you the fightin's over, Daniel. Them Injuns is already gone!"

Faraday saw a slightly glazed look in Britten's eyes. He caught the young agent's other arm and told him, "She's right, Daniel. The battle's done. The Indians have been defeated."

Britten looked at Faraday and gave a shake of his head. Then the look of anger and desperation in his eyes faded. "Mr. Faraday?"

"That's right, son. It's all over."

Callaghan put a big paw on Britten's shoulder. "We run them red scoundrels right back in their hole, Britten. Reckon we hurt 'em so bad they ain't goin' to bother nobody for a while. And we got you to thank for it."

"He was a mite out of his head," Laura said to Faraday and Callaghan. "Said he had to help fight off the Injuns. The doc says he's goin' to be all right, but he needs rest."

"That's right," Faraday nodded. "Come on, Daniel. Let's go back to your tent so you can lie down."

Britten frowned at his employer. "What are you doing here, sir?"

"Time for that later, Daniel. We'll hash it all out. But the trouble is over for now, so you need to rest." Faraday's voice was quiet but insistent.

Britten suddenly jerked his arm out of Faraday's grip. He was staring at something past Faraday's shoulder. "No," Britten said, his voice taut. "It's not over yet."

Faraday turned and followed Britten's gaze. He saw Deborah Rowland and a tall, brawny man striding through the confusion. Behind him, Laura Vint gasped, "There they are!"

Britten pushed between Faraday and Callaghan, moving so quickly that neither of the big men could stop him. Laura was right behind him, looking just as angry and determined. Britten stalked out into a small clearing between tents, and then his voice cut sharply through the cool early-morning air. "Jennings!"

Their backs to Britten, Deborah and the man with her stopped short. Deborah glanced over her shoulder and let out a shriek when she saw Britten and Laura, and with a shudder she broke into a run.

Laura sprang forward, her hand lashing out to grasp the shoulder of Deborah's dress. She set her feet, hauling the other woman around. Laura's work-hardened fist crashed into Deborah's stomach, doubling her over.

Deborah cried out but had the presence of mind to lunge forward, butting at Laura. The two young women grappled, swayed, then fell. Laura landed on top and started punching, battering Deborah with blow after blow.

Faraday and Callaghan glanced at each other, baffled by what was happening but knowing that they could not stand by and watch Deborah be beaten to a pulp. Just as Jennings also decided to take action, they hurried forward, Callaghan grabbing Laura and pulling her off, while Faraday took charge of Deborah. As Faraday helped her to her feet, Deborah recognized him and threw herself against him, sobbing and trembling. Blood streaked her beautiful face.

"Let me go, dammit!" Laura snapped at Callaghan as she wriggled futilely in his grip. "She's part of it, her and that Jennings feller! They set the Injuns on us! They tried to kill Daniel and me!"

Deborah just continued to cry, not denying the

accusations. Jennings's back was turned toward Britten, who stood several yards from him, as Laura continued to make her bitter charges.

Faraday, his craggy face grim, lifted Deborah's chin. He said, "Is it true, Deborah?"

A fresh spasm of sobs wracked her slender body, but she nodded. Faraday glanced at Callaghan again and saw the understanding in the big scout's eyes. A lot of things were becoming clear now.

Britten looked around at the men who now formed a loose circle around him and Jennings—men who had defended the camp with their lives, men with cuts and bullet wounds and dirty faces. He saw Osgood Newton, the draftsman, and Arbuthnot, the surveyor. In the time he had been there at the railhead, those men and others like them had become his friends. And one man's treachery had threatened them all.

"I'm waiting, Jennings," Britten said flatly.

Terence Jennings took a deep breath. Slowly he pivoted to face Britten. Surprisingly there was a smile on his face. Meeting Britten's eyes, he said softly, "I was going to be a rich man."

And his hand darted toward his gun.

Jennings's pistol cleared the holster, the barrel tilting up and lining on Britten as his finger tightened on the trigger. Then the Colt in Daniel Britten's hand blasted, the slug smacking into Jennings's chest and knocking him back two steps. The gun slipped from Jennings's fingers, dropping in the dust as he swayed for a moment before falling on his side. He gasped once, then was still and quiet.

Britten slipped the borrowed Colt back in its holster. He was suddenly very tired. A little sleep sounded like such a good idea. . . .

Callaghan's arm went around Britten's shoulders and held him up, and Britten saw Faraday grinning at him. "I can prove he was guilty," Britten whispered. "I think the telegrapher here in the camp must have been working for him, too. I can explain all of it—"

Dizziness struck him, and he would have fallen had it not been for Sam Callaghan's support.

"Later," Matthew Faraday told him. "Later, Daniel."

More than a week had passed when Matthew Faraday and Daniel Britten returned to the Rowland mansion on the outskirts of Kansas City. This time they were not going to attend a party.

Far from it, Britten thought. This time Deborah Rowland was arriving with them.

In the days that had passed since the escape from the Indian camp and the battle at the railhead, Britten had filled Faraday in on all that he had learned. In return Faraday had explained to his young operative about their new mission for the government. The telegrapher, Marston, had indeed proven to be in the pay of Terence Jennings, but that had been no obstacle. With Faraday working the telegraph key, messages had passed back and forth between Washington and end-of-track for hours on end as the detective explained the case to the authorities. Edward Gentry had assured Faraday that he would send men on the first train to take charge of things at the railhead.

While Faraday was clearing up the details of the case, Britten rested for the most part, being nursed back to health by Laura Vint. Laura had suffered no injuries more serious than cuts and scratches during the ordeal at the Indian camp, and Britten could not have wished for a more gentle, caring nurse.

He had a feeling that she was going to be much more than that to him.

Once Britten was up to traveling, Laura had returned to Kansas City with Faraday and him. With her grandfather dead, she had nothing to keep her on the frontier, and Britten was more than willing to help her start a new life.

Faraday had watched the developing romance with interest, all the while hoping he would not lose Britten as an agent. The young man had proven to be quite capable.

As the carriage neared the front of the Rowland mansion, Faraday brought it to a stop. Britten, sitting beside him, was holding himself a little stiffly because of his injuries. Behind them on the rear seat rode Deborah Rowland, her face downcast and her features shaded under the brim of the hat she wore.

Faraday stepped down from the carriage and then helped Deborah while Britten disembarked from the other side. A groom appeared to take charge of the team. With Deborah between them, Faraday and Britten walked to the front door. Faraday lifted the heavy knocker and brought it down sharply on the wood.

The door was opened a moment later by Hester Rowland, wearing a traveling suit and carrying a pair of gloves in one hand. Her lovely face was pale, her features drawn. When she saw who was standing there, her mouth opened in a circle of surprise.

"Mama . . ." Deborah began brokenly. The young woman started to take a step forward but then stopped, and for several moments the four of them stood unmoving, uncertain of what would happen next. Then Hester Rowland opened her arms and drew her daughter into her embrace.

Meeting Faraday's eyes over Deborah's shoulder, Hester said softly, "Thank you."

Faraday's face was grim, but a trace of gentleness appeared around his mouth and in his eyes. "No charges have been filed against your daughter, Hester," he said. "The authorities and I agree that no real purpose would be served by it. She belongs back here . . . with you."

Hester nodded. With one hand she motioned to someone behind her, then moved aside so that a pair of servants could begin bringing trunks through the doorway.

"You're leaving?" Britten asked in surprise.

With one arm still around Deborah, Hester nodded.

She looked at Faraday and said, "I thought long and hard about what you said to me, Matthew. There really is no reason for me to stay any longer, is there?"

Faraday shook his head. "I don't think so."

"I'll take Deborah with me," Hester declared, more strength in her voice than Faraday had heard there since meeting her again. "She's my daughter, and she needs help. I'll do my best to give it to her."

Faraday glanced at Britten and saw the agreement in the young agent's eyes. Deborah would not go unpunished—she would have to live with the knowledge that she contributed to many deaths, from the first agent sent in by the government to the railroad workers who were killed in the various Indian raids instigated by Terence Jennings.

Another carriage had been brought up, followed closely by a wagon, onto which Hester's luggage was loaded. She said to Deborah, "I had your things packed, too, dear. Come along."

Drawing on her gloves and settling a hat on her blond hair, Hester led her daughter to the carriage.

Faraday stopped her with a question. "Hester, where's Amos?"

Before she could reply, the object of Faraday's question appeared in the mansion's entrance. Amos Rowland was unshaven, his eyes were red-rimmed, and his expensive clothes were disheveled. The odor of whiskey preceded him.

"Hester!" he shouted hoarsely. "You can't do this, Hester! You're my wife, dammit!"

"Good-bye, Amos," Hester said coolly.

"Deborah! Come here, girl. Come here to your father."

Deborah did not look at him but shuddered slightly and climbed into the carriage after her mother.

"All right, go!" Rowland shrieked after them. "You never did understand, damn you! Never understood any of it—" He noticed Faraday and Britten then, as Hester's driver flicked the reins and the carriage began to roll away down the driveway. Pointing a shaking finger at Faraday, Rowland snapped, "You! This is all your fault, Faraday. You bastard!"

With a dangerous smile on his face, Faraday said quietly, "I thrashed you once, Amos. I'd be glad to do it again. You're as much to blame for all of this as anybody. You drove your daughter right into Jennings's arms with your drunken brutality—and he took full advantage of the situation."

Rowland slashed a hand through the air. "No! It wasn't my fault! None of it was my fault!"

Faraday turned away from him. "Come on, Daniel. We're through here."

As they drove away, Amos Rowland stood in front of his mansion, screaming curses and bitterly protesting his innocence. But no one was there any longer to pay any attention to him.

Epilogue

THE KANSAS PACIFIC LOST THE GREAT RACE TO COMPLETE A transcontinental railroad, despite the best efforts of the men who struggled to build it. Eventually it was absorbed into the Union Pacific line, which, on May 10, 1869, met the Central Pacific at Promontory Point, Utah. When the final golden spike had been driven, the dream became reality.

Amos Rowland was not there.

His life ruined by his drinking and the loss of his family, his fortune long gone, he had vanished somewhere in the slums of the East by the time that fateful day arrived.

Watch for

COLLISION COURSE

*next in the Faraday series
coming in September from
Lynx Books!*